SECRETS AND ALCHEMY

DRAGON'S GIFT THE POTION MASTER

LINSEY HALL

For all of the nurses and doctors who are on the front lines fighting to keep us safe.

1

Sora, Void Mage (Kinda)
  Guild City, Hidden within London

Breaking into the lair of the most powerful crime lord in Guild City was easily the most dangerous thing I would ever do.

Also, the coolest.

Fortunately, I was the best magical thief in this city.

Or at least, not the worst. Easily mediocre. I was a solid B and proud of it. Because there were a lot of thieves who were worse than me out there.

In fairness, those other thieves were smart enough not to break into the Devil of Darkvale's secret storehouse of smuggled magical spells and potions. But not me. Nope—nothing would stop me. Not even good sense. Because I needed this payday.

The wizard who wanted this potion had promised to give me a spell that would help me control my magic, and I'd spent years trying to get my hands on that.

Now was my chance, and I wasn't going to let a little thing like possible dismemberment stop me.

I jimmied my lock picks in the keyhole, trying to ignore the cold sweat working its way down my neck. Dawn was creeping toward the horizon, making the air chill and silent. Not that a little thing like the sun would stop a vampire as powerful as the Devil.

"Come on, hurry up," I muttered, glancing down at the unconscious guard who lay at my feet.

He'd been an easy target. Dudes like him never saw me coming. I'd put on my littlest dress, teased my hair, and messed up my makeup so that the mascara bled around my eyes and my lipstick was a smudge of hot pink.

Drunk girl after the walk of shame—or victory, as far as I was concerned. Total non-threat. I stumbled up to him, flirted in a really awkward way, then dosed him with a knock-out potion.

Now he lay at my feet, and I was almost into the Devil's storehouse.

Regardless of what it looked like, I wasn't a total idiot. This wasn't the Devil's main lair that I was breaking into. Hell, no. I'd chosen a satellite storage location at the outskirts of Guild City, near some of the seedier bars. It was supposed to be secret, but I was good at learning secrets.

Cold rain began to fall as I worked, but it was no match

for the cold chill of fear that skated up my spine. The rain felt positively warm compared to that.

"Witches' tits," I muttered. This was taking too long. No wonder that old bat Rodolfo the Red had tried to get me to do this job for him. Wizards were nothing if not clever.

Finally, the lock *snick*ed.

I itched to shove the door open and race inside. This alley didn't have nearly the cover I liked for a job like this. Someone could stroll down the alley any minute and see me—a girl in a minidress and leather jacket trying to break into the Devil of Darkvale's storehouse. That would *definitely* trigger some alarm bells that would then trigger my immediate demise.

Instead, I withdrew the picks and shoved them into my jacket pocket.

The next step of this operation would be to ensure that I didn't get zapped by any protective magic. Since my gifts started and stopped at creating voids, I'd need some help for that.

Fortunately, my thief arsenal was pretty well stocked. I dug a curse breaker out of my pocket. The shiny silver stone felt cold and heavy in my hand as I ran it around the door frame, making sure not to touch the wood. Near the upper right corner of the door, the curse breaker began to vibrate.

"Jackpot." I tapped the silver stone three times against the wood, and magic popped from the curse breaker, vibrating as a light electric shock against my palm.

I grinned.

It had worked.

I kissed the curse breaker. "You haven't failed me yet, old friend."

If someone had called me out on referring to a rock as a friend, well, they wouldn't have been wrong—it was weird. But I loved my curse breaker like a sister. It got me into—and out of—all kinds of trouble.

With the protective enchantment on the door broken, I was able to open it without getting fried. Quickly, I slipped into the dark corridor and turned, snagging the unconscious guard by the collar and heaving him into the corridor behind me.

I propped him against the wall and patted his cheek. "There now, you'll be fine. Enjoy your nap."

Quickly, I shut the door and flicked on a light switch, illuminating a narrow hall punctuated by eight closed doors.

"Damn. That's a lot of freaking doors." I had no idea which one led to the potions storeroom.

Heart pounding, I hurried down the hall, peeking into each room as I ran. Rare books, check. Weapons, check. Strange plants, check. One room that was filled with scary pink mist, check.

I didn't know what the Devil got up to, exactly, but I knew it was dangerous, illegal shit. The stuff in these rooms was worth millions, and I couldn't deny that just looking at it gave me itchy fingers.

"Focus, dumbbell," I muttered.

Finally, I found the room full of potions. Shelves lined

the walls, each stacked with tiny bottles of gleaming liquid. I scanned the different bottles, searching for the distinctive golden gleam of the potion that Rodolfo had requested. Apparently, the Expulsio potion was *really* valuable. Even the Devil might not know what he had stored in there.

I did.

Well, at least, I kind of did. I knew it was valuable, anyway. And that it was my ticket to fixing my wonky magic.

There!

My gaze snagged on the gleaming golden vial sitting at head height on the other side of the room. I ran toward it, doing pretty well in my heels, if I did say so myself. Part of successful thievery was really committing to the disguise, you know? So I was in stilettos for this job. Even my hair was messy, as if I'd had a long, hard night hanging on to the bar at the Drunken Pixie. The guard had totally fallen for it, and then *I'd* felled *him*.

I stopped in front of the shelf and peered hard at the golden vial. Within, tiny flecks of silver gleamed.

"Bingo." I grinned. "You're *just* what I was looking for."

From down the hall, a shuffling sounded.

My skin iced.

Guards.

Not the one I'd knocked out—he'd be unconscious for another hour, at least. Other guards.

More than one.

Oh, witches' tits.

I couldn't be caught down here.

Heart thundering so loud it nearly deafened me, I grabbed the vial of gold potion from the shelf. It sparked against my hand, a protective charm stinging wildly. Tears smarted as I fought not to drop the vial.

Should have taken the time to use the curse breaker.

"Hey! What are you doing here?" a deep voice demanded from behind me.

Jig's up.

I spun fast, mind racing. There were at least three guards, each of them armed with a bat that sparked with magic. Panic flared, so sharp and fierce that I felt a kinship with all the rats who'd ever been caught in traps. My gaze zeroed in on their bats. Blue magic flickered like neon ice.

I couldn't fight that.

I couldn't fight much of anything, in fact.

I was sneaky, not tough. *And* I was wearing stilettos.

Fear made my magic pulse inside me, rising up from the pit of my soul. I used it rarely—only when the alternative was basically death.

The lead guard growled and stepped forward. He raised the bat, and my gaze followed the sparking wood.

Oh, gargoyle balls. That would hurt.

Fear added gasoline to my magic, igniting it within me. An overwhelming desire to protect myself roared to life, and I raised my hand, my magic surging through me.

I had to take the risk.

The magic blasted out of me, and I tried to direct it toward the guards, praying that the void would devour their weapons and knock them out. My gift was a weird one, capable of making things disappear when I wanted it to. If it hit a living being, the shock usually knocked them unconscious, which was *exactly* what I needed right now.

As soon as the magic left my fingertips, I could feel it—something was wrong.

The power exploded all around me, the sucking sensation of the void pulling at my skin. I screamed, panic flaring, and gripped the potion tight.

But the void pulled hard, yanking the potion from my grip. As I collapsed, I felt my clothes tear away. Chill air rushed over me as I hit the ground hard.

Fear chilled me, the only thing tethering me to awareness. Barely conscious, I spotted the three guards through bleary eyes.

They stood, staring down at me with shock on their faces.

I tried to sit up, but my muscles felt like water. Out of the corner of my eye, I spotted my empty hand. The hand that had once held the potion.

It was gone.

Along with my minidress, jacket, and shoes. I hoped the void hadn't gotten my underwear, but it was impossible to say.

The guards strode up to me, and fear fought within my chest, scratching at my ribs like a trapped animal.

A grimace twisted the biggest guard's face. "Joey, put your coat on her."

"Come on, Clyde," the man to his right moaned. Had to be Joey. "This is a new coat. My old lady got it for me."

"Boss won't like it if we bring her in like this." He nudged my hip with his foot, and I had the terrible feeling that I was totally naked.

The terrified animal inside my chest turned into an elephant, nearly stomping my organs. I was so weak I couldn't even move—even now, I fought for consciousness. The things they could do to me…

Joey groaned again and stripped off his jacket, bending down to force me into it.

Was he keeping his eyes averted?

It was hard to say, given how woozy I was. My vision was really fading out, and it was making me nauseous.

Oh, dragon dick.

I lurched forward and puked all over Joey's shoes.

His vicious curse was the last thing I heard.

~

"Wake up." The sharp voice was so cold that I swore it turned my tits into a witch's.

Blearily, I blinked my eyes open.

At first, the room swam hazily in my vision. I swallowed hard, trying not to puke again, and realized that I was tied to a chair. I tilted my head down to inspect myself, my head pounding.

I wore a man's jacket zipped up all the way to my neck. It was long enough to cover the important bits, but the cold chair under my ass confirmed my fear.

I *had* been naked.

My wonky freaking void magic had sucked away the Expulsio potion *and* my clothes.

But the big thing right now was my former nakedness. And the fact that I'd been unconscious with three goons.

My heart began to thunder, and a cold sweat broke out over my skin. The guards. *Had they, had they...*

I couldn't even process the words, it was so terrible to think about what could have happened.

"They didn't touch you." The cold voice was soft but certain. As if the owner could read my thoughts and wanted to reassure me, but wasn't going to waste any extra breath on being nice about it. As if it were a point of pride that his goons didn't rape girls.

My gaze snapped up to the figure sitting behind the massive desk. I could make out two huge guards standing in the shadows behind him. Shifters, probably. They usually provided security detail in Guild City. All that shit about being strong, brave, and dutiful, or whatever. They had a Latin motto for it, but I didn't know what it was.

But the man himself was a blur. It took a moment for my hazy vision to clear, but when it did...hoo boy.

If he weren't so terrifying, the Devil would be a major hottie. He looked like he'd been born from an artist's chisel and a block of marble. Just as cold looking, too, with his dark hair, eerie silver eyes, and perfect features.

He was cold, though, like ice that chilled the air around him, and it disturbed me.

He sprawled elegantly in a chair behind the desk, his posture relaxed but his gaze intense. He had the air of someone who could spring into action at a moment's notice—and when he did, you'd be dead.

Though it was impossible to see all of him behind the desk, it was clear that he was tall and leanly muscled, his entire being screaming *deadly*. Every inch of him looked like he could find a creative way to kill you with it. Like he wanted to hold the Guinness World Record for Most Murders by Pinky and Other Seemingly Nonthreatening Body Parts.

The guards behind him were just to do the dirty work. The Devil himself was the deadly one.

Except he was all self-control. I could see it like an aura around him. This man never lost his temper, but it didn't mean he wasn't the most dangerous person in this city.

"You've got the wrong girl." I hoped he couldn't hear my heartbeat.

"You knocked yourself out on my secure property while trying to steal from me." He raised a perfect brow, and something about it made me uncomfortable.

I could see the damage on this guy. I'd heard the stories —he'd made himself up from nothing and had the dark and terrible past to prove it.

"There are consequences for stealing from me." He toyed with a pen on his desk, and my gaze followed the movements, cold fear running through me.

I could imagine him strangling me with those hands and not even breaking a sweat.

My gaze flicked up to his, finding his cold silver eyes

staring into me. Was he putting that vision in my head to scare me?

I jerked my gaze away from him. "I didn't steal."

"Not for lack of trying. And the result is the same…the Expulsio potion is gone. Where did you send it?"

"Ah…" *Witches' tits.* I hadn't sent it anywhere. I had no idea where things went when the void took them. I'd freaking lost it.

"You lost it."

Gargoyle balls, I'm bad at this.

"No. Not lost." I grinned. "I swear, it's not lost. I sent it away."

"And you can get it back?" His too-sharp eyes watched me.

"Yep. If you let me go, I will get it back."

"Lies."

"No, not lies." I shook my head, mind racing. "I can totally get it back. I swear."

He tilted his head, expression considering. "I think you're willing to try."

"Does this mean you won't kill me?" I asked, my heartbeat thundering so loud it nearly deafened me.

"I'm not sure." He sighed. "I want my property returned more than I want your head."

"I think that's great." I nodded, sending him a blinding smile. "And I can do that for you." All I had to do was get out of there and run for it.

"Running for it isn't an option, you know."

My jaw tightened. Could he read minds?

"If you don't bring me that potion, you'll never be allowed back in Guild City." He leaned forward. "I control the gates. There's no in or out without my knowledge."

I swallowed hard, the truth of his words sinking in. I could run, but not far enough to escape him. I lived in Guild City, the most amazing place in the world. The ancient walled city was hidden deep in the historic heart of London—a place that blended the Old World and New. Some said it had been founded by the Devil of Darkvale hundreds of years ago. They even said he was Vlad the Impaler, but I didn't know if any of that was true.

What I *did* know was that it was my home, and I couldn't live anywhere but here. The wild, crazy place full of magic and mystery flowed in my veins, and if I somehow managed to escape, never being able to return would kill me.

And the Devil owned it all.

Not literally, but enough of it that he could destroy my life here.

And from the ice in his eyes, it was clear that he would be willing to.

"I don't want to leave." My words rang with truth. I really didn't. "But I'll need to, in order to get your potion back."

"And how do I know that you will return?"

"Put a tracker on me." I couldn't believe I was saying that. If I allowed that, he could find me anywhere and kill me.

But if I didn't succeed and could never again return to

Guild City—that would kill me as well. Just more slowly and painfully.

He frowned, clearly interested. "All right. And where will you go from there?"

"To the Alchemist. I'll get you your potion back, I swear."

2

Connor

Magic's Bend, Oregon

In the cauldron, the potion sizzled. Pale blue smoke wafted up, reeking of brimstone and death. I turned my head to the side, breathing shallowly through my mouth.

This wasn't the first time I'd brewed a potion that made me want to hurl, and it wouldn't be the last.

For one, the price was right.

But mostly, the wizard who needed it was losing his memory faster every day.

Poor bastard. I'd hate to go that way, and I'd do what I could to help a fellow Magica.

Carefully, I stirred the slender silver spoon. It looked out of place in my big, scarred hands, but I'd learned to be careful with tiny tasks.

A pounding echoed from the front of my bar, Potions & Pastilles. I frowned, glancing up at the clock on the wall. The pale white face was nearly hidden behind dozens of jars piled on the shelf right beneath it, but I could see that it was past three a.m.

"Who the hell is knocking at this hour?"

It was too late for the night owls who came for whiskey and too early for the coffee regulars. I ran Potions & Pastilles as a combo coffee shop and bar, and while I enjoyed it, it was primarily a front for my potions business. I made things that were so rare and deadly—and expensive—that it was good to have a front for the operation.

The Order of the Magica—our local government in Magic's Bend—liked to ask too many questions. And I didn't want to answer. Better that they know nothing.

And hell, over the years, I'd grown to like the work. There was something soothing about making lattes after a long night of brewing up deadly potions. Even the worst latte wouldn't blow your head off.

The pounding sounded louder, and I scowled, killing the flame beneath the cauldron and turning to leave my lab. The place was silent tonight, my sister having recently moved into her boyfriend's place. Technically, they were fated mates—it was a Fae thing that I was skeptical of, since I'd long ago renounced my Fae heritage—but they were definitely the real deal.

At the thought of the Fae, my hand went to my pocket, where a tiny vial of potion always sat. If I drank it, it would give me back my wings.

I'd been carrying it around for years, unwilling to take it. First, because my sister didn't have her wings, and it wouldn't fix her. I wouldn't leave her in the dust.

But the main reason was that once I took the potion, it would begin a deadly transition. When I'd given up my wings, I'd also given up powerful magic. It'd been easy. But getting it back? That could be deadly. And taking the potion was just the first part. The second part: it was so unlikely I'd survive that it had never seemed worth it.

Not to mention the dreams...

Every time I thought of my lost powers, I saw an unknown Fae village burning. It was enough to keep me away.

The banging on the front door increased, and I shoved the thoughts away. Quickly, I cut through the long kitchen toward the swinging door that led to the main part of the bar. I pushed it open and stepped into the darkened interior of P&P, stopping behind the counter that separated the work area from the seating area.

It was so dark in here that the streetlights outside made the woman on the other side of the glass seem to glow. Her golden hair was pulled back, and though I couldn't make out her features, I could tell that she was dressed in jeans and a T-shirt.

Even from this far away, the sight of her hit me in the gut like a demon's punch. My breath seemed to leave my body.

Her.

What the hell? I rubbed a hand over my jaw, feeling the slight stubble that came from a long night in the lab.

"Hey!" her voice sounded through the glass. "Come on. Open up!"

I blinked at her, head still reeling. I'd *never* felt this way about a woman before.

But it was like something in me tugged me toward her, a wire that tightened, trying to draw us nearer. I shook the thought away and strode out from behind the bar.

As I neared, it was easier to see her delicate features through the glass doors. Full lips, big dark eyes, straight nose.

She was a stunner.

I'd never considered myself to be a guy with a type before, but suddenly I was. And it was *her*.

Quickly, I unlatched the door and swung it open.

The first thing that struck me was her scent—lilacs. It wasn't the scent of her magic, though. It was just the scent of *her*. And damned if I didn't like it.

I was drawing it into my lungs when her hand slammed into my chest and she shoved me back into the bar. Heat shot from the spot where her hand pressed against me, and I did my best to ignore it.

"Hey, watch it," I said.

She kept pushing as I stumbled back, then withdrew her hand.

Immediately, I felt a sense of loss. Everything in me screamed to pull her toward me and kiss her, but that was ridiculous. I'd just met her.

She spun and shut the door behind her, then locked it.

"Someone after you?" I asked. Protectiveness surged inside me, a sensation I'd only ever felt with my sister and a few of my closest friends.

But there was something about it that was more…more primal. Intense. Compelling.

She turned back to me and crossed her arms. "*You're the Alchemist?*"

"Potion Master."

"Potato, potahto." She looked me up and down. "You're just…not what I was expecting, Mr. Alchemist."

"What were you expecting?"

She shrugged. "I don't know. Little reedy guy? Good with his hands?"

"I'm *very* good with my hands."

"Suuuure." Despite her tone, there was definitely interest in her voice. And suddenly, I was pretty damned interested in convincing her. She gestured to me. "It's just that you're so…big."

I glanced at the decorative mirror to my right, catching sight of myself. She wasn't wrong. I loomed over her, my shoulders broad underneath my worn T-shirt.

"Checking yourself out?" she asked, a smile in her voice.

"Checking you out." I turned back to her, feeling a matching grin stretch across my face.

She raised a brow. "So, that's how it's going to be."

I shrugged. "Not very often I have a beautiful woman show up on my doorstep at three a.m."

"Well, get those thoughts out of your head. I want to hire you."

"For what?" My gaze swept her form again, searching for an aura or any other hint of her magical signature. Weirdly, she was pretty much a black hole. "What are you, anyway? I can't get a sense of it, and I'm not keen on working for someone I can't identify."

She scoffed. "We don't all walk around with our signatures hanging out, you know."

"Yeah, but even people who are suppressing theirs clearly have *some* touch of magic." I drew in a breath, but I only got the scent of lilacs. No magic. "And you must have some, if you're here in Magic's Bend."

"Don't worry, I'm not a sneaky human who somehow wandered past the wards of your fair hamlet."

"Then what are you?"

"None of your business. I'm nothing sinister. It's just that where I come from, we keep our signatures on the down-low. All of us."

"And where do you come from?"

"Not sure I want to tell you that. Not until I get your agreement to help me."

I'd help her.

Immediately, I knew I'd help her.

Not that I wanted her to know that. Talk about laying all your cards on the table. I didn't even know her name, but I was pretty sure I wanted her to marry me.

"What do you need?"

"An Expulsio potion."

A laugh escaped me. "Really, what do you need?"

"I just told you."

Damn it. She was being serious. I raked a hand through my hair. "Those things are almost impossible to find ingredients for. You got them?"

"No."

"Know where to get them?"

"No." She shrugged. "Well, maybe. I don't know what's in an Expulsio potion. But if you tell me, maybe I can get the stuff. I know some people."

"Why do you need it so bad?" Expulsios were damned valuable. They could be used to wipe memories or create new ones. "I'm not keen on making it for someone I don't even know."

She frowned, and her gaze moved left, away from mine.

"You look shifty."

She scowled at me. "I do not."

"How about you start by telling me your name?"

She frowned. "I didn't do that, did I?"

"No. You just jumped into what you needed, which makes me think you're in trouble."

"Am not."

"Oh, my gods, you're a terrible liar."

She scowled at me, and it was so cute I wanted to hug her.

Whoa. That was weird. Totally not a thought I normally had about women I'd just met.

"Come on, you can tell me." I raised my hands,

gesturing to the coffee shop around me. "I'll even make you a drink. Whiskey or coffee?"

"Both?"

"Irish coffee, coming right up." I turned, striding quickly back to the bar. I wanted to give her some space, and hell, *I* needed some space. I looked back at her. "But you need to tell me your name."

"Sora."

A frisson of *something* raced over me. Like things finally falling into place. I shook it away. Crazy. "I'm Connor."

"Hi, Connor."

It didn't take me long to make the coffee, but I chose straight whiskey for myself. I handed her drink to her, and the way she clutched it had the slightest air of desperation to it.

She grabbed it the way you'd grab a glass of wine at a dinner party with your asshole boss, or a glass of whiskey after you'd witnessed a murder.

Something had happened to her, and I found myself wanting to fix it.

∼

Sora

The hot alchemist stared at me with real concern in his dark eyes—like real, actual, concern.

He looked like some kind of fantasy version of a bad

boy rocker who made magic potions with his big, sexy hands and bench-pressed refrigerators for fun. He had the kind of muscles that were built in battle, and I couldn't keep my eyes off his arms. Which was really shallow of me, but... Not all of my moments were proud ones.

He was worlds different than the Devil of Darkvale —*my* kind of different.

Just as hot, just as deadly, but with a core of goodness that I'd be able to see from a mile away. Both men possessed the same icy control, but whereas the Devil was an actual icicle, this guy could thaw. And when he did, he'd be *hot*.

But mostly, it was just that he reminded me of Captain America with dark hair, and I'd always been into superheroes. And his faint British accent reminded me of home, which I liked.

Which was how I ended up spilling the whole story to him, leaving out only the fact that I possessed wonky void magic. *That* I would save for another day. People were generally scared of me since I could, like, make them disappear and stuff.

When I finally wound down, I stared at him.

Oh, my goblin guts.

I could not believe I'd just spilled all of that to him.

Motormouth? Check!

I grinned weakly. "So, you wanna help?"

He leaned back, his broad shoulders stretching his T-shirt. There was a dark gray emblem on it that I couldn't identify, but he spoke before I could ask about it, his vaguely British accent very light, as if he'd lived here for years and had mostly adopted an American way of speaking. "You're saying you stole from the most dangerous person in Guild City?"

"You've heard of him?"

"Sure. Never met him, though."

"Ever been to Guild City?"

"No reason to go." He raked a hand through his longish dark hair, the muscles of his forearm cording and creating shadows that made my mouth water. Two thick leather cuffs encircled his wrists, and they looked like there might be tiny glass vials built into them on the inside.

I wanted to ask about them, but I needed to focus on getting his help first. "If you help me, I'll give you a tour."

"Not sure I want to go somewhere owned by a guy like that."

"I'll make it a beer tour."

"Like a date?" He raised his eyebrows again, clearly interested.

"Could be." He was just as far out of my league as the Devil, but at least Connor was playing a game I wanted to join. I leaned closer, propping my arms on the bar and trying to ignore the amazing smell of his skin. Soap and evergreen.

Not to mention his magic.

Hoo boy, these Magic's Bend folks sure let their magic all hang out. That would never be allowed in Guild City. The Council of the Guilds—London's Magical Government—had decreed that all citizens keep their magic on extreme lockdown, since our little town was hidden inside a bigger human city. It'd do us no favors to have a ton of magic seething around the place.

This guy, though. His magic smelled like whiskey and felt like a warm hug. Tasted like good chocolate and sounded like a river rushing downstream.

And he was hot enough to melt *both* sets of my panties. I'd put on an extra pair since my magic had eaten my last ones in front of three strangers. It was a weird way of coping, but hey, it was mine.

Yeah, I liked him.

In an *I want to jump your bones* kind of way.

"Why did you try to steal it?" he asked.

"I needed it."

"That's a terrible answer." He dragged a hand down his face, his eyes wary but interested.

"It's all I've got. But I promise I wasn't going to do anything terrible with it." I tried to force my sincerity toward him, tried to make him believe me by my voice alone.

It seemed to satisfy him—or at least, he was still curious enough not to kick me out—because he asked, "So, if you bring this potion to the mob boss, he'll let you return to your home?"

I nodded. "Yep."

"And do you know what he's going to do with the potion?"

"No."

"Do you care?"

"Kind of?" I shrugged. "The Devil of Darkvale is powerful. Dangerous. Deadly. I don't want to get on his bad side. But he's got...rules."

"What kind of rules?"

"He'll only hurt—like, *really* hurt—those who are as powerful as he is. Or evil. Trust me, there are way worse people in Guild City than him."

"And yet, you're still scared of him."

"Hell, yeah. Because I'm not an idiot. He'd ruin my life, no problem." I shivered at the thought of being kicked out of my only home.

"So how does he make his money if he's so picky? Isn't all the money in the bad stuff?"

"Depends on how you define 'bad.' I think for the Devil, it's smuggling, mostly. Guild City has more regulations than you do here. He makes a mint getting around them. Sells magic, booze, access to power and status. He has everything he needs to make my life a living hell."

"Fine. I'll help you. But how did you find me, if you're all the way over in Guild City?"

I scoffed. "Everyone knows about you, Alchemist."

"No one calls me 'Alchemist.'"

"I do, because it's sexy." I couldn't believe my mouth. Flirting like this! But it was fun.

"We'll come back to that sexy bit later. And we will *definitely* come back to it. But first, I want to know what I'm going to get out of this deal."

"Besides the tour of Guild City?"

"You were serious?"

"Yeah. Guild City is *nice*. And not just anyone gets to visit."

He gave me a skeptical look. "As nice as that sounds... I want more. How about a trade? What's your species?"

I glared at him.

"You're really not going to tell me your species?"

"What if I'm a hedgehog shifter and I'm embarrassed?"

"Oh, come on. Hedgehogs are adorable."

I laughed. "Not in a fight."

"I don't know. Those quills could do some damage."

"Sure." I studied Connor, wanting to turn the conversation around. He had so much magic, his signatures nearly overwhelming.

But there was something else about him...

Something about his magic that wasn't quite complete.

Like me?

A frisson of excitement shot through me. Obviously, he was an insanely skilled potions master—I'd heard his name all the way over in Guild City. But was he like me a little bit, with a touch of wonky magic?

"Something about your signature is weird," I said. "Incomplete."

Shadows crossed his face, and I almost regretted the words. But I couldn't stop them from coming out. I had to know. "Seriously, dude. What is it? Magic a bit broken?"

"I've got some wings that I don't claim." He shrugged. "What about you? I showed you mine, now you show me yours."

A tiny huff of laughter escaped me. "You showed me

barely anything."

"Ask only a little of me, and I'll ask only a little of you."

I sighed. Hiding it this hard was making things weird. And I liked the idea that he wouldn't ask details. Sure, it was as a way to protect his own secrets, but that was something we had in common. "I'm a Void Mage. So unless you want some magical disposal done, I can't help you much."

He leaned back and tapped one hand against his bicep, clearly thinking. My gaze was riveted to the unconscious display of strength. Hey, what could I say? I was easy.

"I don't really need any magical disposal done," he said. "But you'd come in handy in a big fight, if you could void the other side's weapons."

"Yes, I'd be fantastic at that." I nodded, knowing my eyes were a bit bright and hoping he didn't catch on to the fact that I was lying through my teeth. "Let's do that."

He nodded, clearly satisfied.

Relief flooded through me. I was on my way to fixing this, thank fates.

But I was totally ignoring the fact that I currently had no way to get the spell that would restore my magic. I'd originally been stealing the Expulsio potion to give it to Rodolfo the Red. Now I was trying to get it remade to replace the one I'd broken so that the Devil of Darkvale wouldn't come after me, but that left me up shit creek regarding my magic.

"Actually..." I eyed him hopefully. "Could you make two Expulsio potions?"

"Why?"

My mind raced. "It would get me in the Devil's good graces."

His eyes narrowed suspiciously, and I smiled, hoping it looked not-weird. I didn't want to admit that I needed the second potion to fix my wonky magic. It was hard enough to make friends when they knew I could lose control of my power and blast them.

And I liked him.

He wouldn't want to be around me if he thought I could blast him by mistake. And there was no way a guy like him knew what it was like to have magic you couldn't use. Sure, I'd asked if his magic was a bit broken, but there was no way that was true. He was just too...powerful and perfect. He'd never be able to relate.

He leaned forward, propping his muscular arms on the table. As he caught my eye, the whiskey and evergreen scent of him swept over me. "Say I take the favor deal. I want something else, too."

I swallowed hard. "What?"

"A date."

"A date?" I nearly squeaked the words.

"Yeah. Presuming this thing between us"—he gestured at the air between us as if he were pointing to an actual wire that tied us together—"is still there when we're done getting this potion made. I want a date."

Hell, yeah.

Nope—I had to play it cool.

I crossed my arms over my chest and nodded. "We'll see."

3

Connor

"Good enough for me." I leaned back, pleased that I'd snagged a possible date with the hot not-hedgehog.

Who might also be my mate.

If I believed in such Fae things. Which I should, given that I was technically Fae. But I was still wrestling with how much I actually wanted to *be* Fae.

"What do we do next?" Sora asked.

"There's at least one ingredient in that potion that I've never even seen before. Never had access to."

"You know the ingredients by heart?"

"Why do you think they call me a Potions *Master*?"

"Whatever, Alchemist."

"That doesn't make me sound any less knowledgeable or cool, you know."

"Yeah, you have a point." She pulled out her cell phone. "I might know some people who can help us get the ingredient you need. What's it called?"

"Powdered Ascencia root."

"That a tree?"

"Flower. Very delicate, and blooms once every ten years."

She whistled low under her breath and started typing into her phone.

"Who are you contacting?"

"A friend at the Witches' Guild. She'll know if they have the ingredient."

"That's what these witches deal in? Magical ingredients?"

"Not really. You're more likely to get ingredients from the Sorcerers' Guild. They have a far bigger stash for their spells. But they'd *never* sell to me."

"Why not?"

"Tried to break in too many times." She grinned devilishly, and I wanted to ask why she'd been breaking in so often. But she spoke before I could. "That's not an option, though. And I'm *not* telling you the story. So that leaves the Witches' Guild. They sell spells and potions, but they need ingredients for those. With any luck, they'll sell us some."

"Works for me." I was actually pretty psyched to see the famed Guild City. Getting inside a guild would be an even bigger coup, as far as magical tourism was concerned.

"What else do we need?" Sora asked.

"Should have everything else in the back." I stood,

intending to go check. Sora rose as well, and I gestured for her to follow. "Come on."

I led her through the kitchens to my lab. It was rare I took someone back there, but I liked her.

As we entered the cluttered room, she whistled low under her breath. "This is quite the setup."

"Not bad, if I do say so myself." I grinned and searched the shelves for the other ingredients, setting them aside. As I was finishing up, her phone buzzed.

Out of the corner of my eye, I could see her pull the cell phone from her pocket and check it. I turned in time to see her shoot me a brilliant smile, and it felt like my heart was about to beat its way out of my chest.

Yeah. There was something about this woman that was special.

Absently, I rubbed the spot right over my heart, as if I could get the feeling to stop.

"Does your friend have the ingredient?" I asked, trying to ignore the Fae sense that this woman was *the one.*

I sure as hell hadn't expected to find my fated mate, but fate seemed to have other ideas.

"Yep. We can head over there now and meet with them." She gave me a look up and down. "How good are you at flirting?"

I shrugged. "All right, I guess?"

"Well, do your best. We'll need to butter them up, because they might not want to part with this ingredient."

"I'll see what I can do." I grabbed a bag and filled it full of potion bombs, then threw in a few healing draughts and some particularly valuable potions in case we needed to make a trade. They were all stored in a glass containers of different shapes and colors, making it easy for me to tell which was which before I threw it.

"What are those for?" she asked.

"In case it gets dicey."

"Those are weapons?"

"Yes." I stashed the potion bag in the ether. It was an expensive magical spell that allowed me to store objects in the ephemeral stuff that filled in the spaces between everything in the world, but it came in damned handy.

I checked the thick leather cuffs around my wrists to make sure that the tiny vials of potion were all full. They were hidden on the inside of my cuffs, close to my skin, and were easy to access in a pinch.

Finished, I looked up at Sora. "How are we getting there?"

She dug into her pocket and pulled out a small stone. "I've got one transport charm left. So if we get in a pinch at the Witches' Guild, we'll have to run for it the old-fashioned way."

"We could get in that kind of a pinch?"

"It's dangerous in there, even if they don't hate me like the Sorcerers' Guild does."

"All right then." I grabbed a couple transport charms from the shelf and put one in my pocket. The other, I kept in my hand. "Hang on to yours. We'll use one of mine."

"Thanks."

I just nodded. I didn't want her to get into a bad situation in the future and not have a quick way out.

I held out my hand so that I could bring her through the ether with me to the right location. "Ready?"

"Ready as a werewolf for the full moon." She gripped my hand, and a flash of heat streaked through me. This was the first time our skin had touched, and it was *electric.*

A small gasp escaped her, and her gaze flicked up to mine.

Yeah, this woman was something to me.

And she had no idea.

I didn't really appreciate fate meddling in my life like this, but that was just the way the world worked.

"We're going to Covent Garden first," she said. "From there, we'll go through the gate into Guild City."

"Sounds good." I handed her the transport charm. "Actually, why don't you envision our location? You'll get us closer to the right place."

She nodded and took it, then closed her eyes as she chucked the transport charm to the ground. A cloud of glittering silver smoke poofed up around us, and she stepped forward, letting it envelop her. I followed, and the ether sucked us in, spinning us through space. It spat us out in the middle of an empty alley.

It was daylight in London, sometime in the midmorning. The air smelled of wet cobblestones, and the clouds hung heavy in the sky.

Sora glanced upward and grimaced. "Another lovely day."

I grinned. Oregon got its fair share of rain, too, but there was something drearier about English cities.

"Come on." She let go of my hand and started down the alley. "There are two main gates that lead into Guild City."

I caught up to her, squeezing alongside her in the narrow alley. "Guild City is in its own realm, right?"

"Basically. When it was formed—about five hundred years ago, now—magic was used to fit it into London without disrupting the human settlement. The humans don't know it's here, but we do."

"And it's only accessible through the gates?"

"Yep. Two of them, both located in Guild City. But there are multiple magical entrance points on the human plane. We're headed to one that's in The Haunted Hound."

"Sounds like a pub. They're open at this hour?"

"They're always open, if you know how to get in." She exited the alley and turned onto a street that was pretty much empty. Most of the shops were shuttered, and I remembered that it was Sunday. They wouldn't open for a few more hours.

Sora strode about ten yards down the street and stopped in front of the most boring store I could imagine: toilet paper. Just....tons of toilet paper, hundreds of white rolls of it. Next to the door, a narrow alley was cluttered with rubbish bins. Sora looked down the street in either direction.

There was no one around except a young woman on the far side of the street, leaning against the wall with a paper cup of takeout coffee. She appeared to be scrolling through her cell phone, her hoodie concealing most of her face. But her gaze occasionally flicked up to us, one brilliant eye visible behind the sweep of hair. Something in her stance suggested the coiled power of someone used to danger. Used to taking care of themselves.

"Coast is clear," Sora said.

"What about that woman back there?"

"I can feel her magic. She's cool. Just worried about humans."

I nodded, but shot the woman another look. There was something strange about her...

Sora entered the alley, drawing my attention. She walked right through the trash cans.

I followed, glancing back at the strange woman one more time.

Her magic...

The signature was powerful. *Very* powerful.

Yet, the lack of control she had over it suggested she didn't even know she had it. Or didn't care.

"You coming?" Sora asked.

Her voice tugged my attention toward her, reminding me that I already had one woman to take care of, and she was the one I really wanted. "Yes."

I followed her deeper into the alley, stepping through the illusion of trash cans and garbage. Despite the fact that it wasn't real, it still reeked, and I held my breath to avoid inhaling the stench.

"Good magic," I said.

She tossed a grin at me over her shoulder. "Yep. They worked extra hard on that stench. Very believable."

"You're telling me. My stomach is turning, and I'm not even inhaling."

Once we were past the trash cans, I spotted a door. The top contained several tiny panes of glass that were so grimy it was impossible to see through them, and the door itself had probably once been red. It was now thoroughly coated in grime.

The sign over it read The Haunted Hound.

It was the least inviting place I'd ever seen.

"Horrible, right?" Sora grinned.

"Very."

"Mac works hard to keep it like this." She pressed her hand to the door, and I could see the faint glitter of magic around her palm. She shot me a look over her shoulder. "Just a charm to make sure only those with magic can enter."

I nodded. It was a common device. "So, anyone with magic can get into Guild City?"

"Anyone with magic can get into the bar. Getting into Guild City requires getting through the gates, and only those with permission are allowed into the city."

"Good thing I'm with you, then."

"Just remember that when things get dicey." She shot me a grin and pushed her way into the bar.

I followed her as she cut through the crowd of people that sat at various high-top tables.

It was a nice place on the inside, despite the exterior.

Dark wood, gleaming golden lamps, a long wooden bar, and framed old beer advertisements on the wall. The low ceiling was studded with dark beams, giving it an ancient vibe that I liked.

Despite the fact that it was still midmorning, the pub was full. People were cluttered around plates of breakfast and hot coffee, with a few mimosas scattered amongst the crowd.

"Every day is brunch day here," Sora said. "Local supernaturals want a place with no humans to hang out."

"These people don't live in Guild City?"

"Unlikely. If they did, they'd be eating there. They live in this neighborhood, which is like an in-between zone. More supernaturals than humans, though they keep their existence on the down-low."

"Gotcha."

Sora cut through the crowd, giving a quick salute to the bartender. The woman manning the taps was tall and slender, with white-blonde hair that suggested she was of Nordic descent. She nodded at Sora, barely spared a glance for me, then went back to drying glasses with a pink cloth.

Sora strode around to the right side of the bar. It was a quieter corner, no doubt because the bathrooms were back there, but she veered toward a plain brown door that looked like the service entrance for the kitchens. Without hesitating, she pressed a hand to the wooden door. Magic sparked around her palm briefly before the door gave way under the pressure and swung open.

She entered a dark corridor, and I followed, magic prickling powerfully off my skin.

One dim lamp hung over the long corridor. Shelves cluttered the walls, but the liquor bottles on them were so dusty that they looked like they hadn't been moved in decades. Closer inspection revealed that they were empty.

"A cover," Sora said. "Meant to look like storage."

"Except they're empty."

"What can I say? Mac is cheap. No one looks too close, anyway."

I nodded, turning back to her. She was standing at the far side of the hall, pressing her hand to the wall. More magic sparked, and she reached back to take my hand. "Come on."

Energy fizzed up my arm as I gripped her palm, the feeling of her skin sending a jolt of awareness through me.

Maybe it was my imagination, but I thought her hand tightened on mine.

Was she feeling it, too?

Because I'd never felt this with another woman. This kind of *knowledge*. An insanely intense attraction that was impossible to deny.

Before I could analyze it any further, she pulled me through the wall. The ether sucked us in, spinning us through space and spitting us into the watery sunlight of the outdoors.

It took my senses a moment to adjust, but one thing was clear: this place reeked of danger.

4

Sora

As soon as I arrived at the gate into Guild City, I felt it.

Danger.

It prickled on the air like sharp little bubbles. Which was the point of the magic, actually. I was *supposed* to feel it and be worried.

The Devil of Darkvale. He wanted me to feel threatened. I stepped nearer to Connor and inspected our surroundings. The gates into Guild City weren't normal little gates. They were large buildings that had been constructed in the medieval period. Both of them were two stories tall, like this one, though the main gate had a huge clock tower over it.

But this tower was big enough, an intimidating building with two conical turrets on top that just screamed

Middle Ages. Parts of the city were more modern, but a lot of it was the same as it had been when it was first built.

Normally, I passed through the gates by pressing my hand to the door so that it could sense my magic and allow me in. Guards did live in the huge gatehouse building, but they didn't monitor every person who entered. The gate itself did a good enough job of that, only allowing in magical beings with prior permission to be there. The guards were there for special circumstances, like human guests (super rare), unwelcome Magica, and in the rare cases that the city was under attack.

That hadn't happened in decades, though.

Connor and I stood just outside of the gatehouse, the massive wooden door shut in our face. There were two doors, however. The larger one was so big that a lorry could drive through it. Not that a lorry *would* drive through it. It'd be impossible to get it through the entryways on the human plane. And Guild City was a pedestrian town, anyway, though there were some motorcycles.

The large gate was rarely used, however. To the right was the smaller door that saw a lot more foot traffic. It swung open, and one of the Devil's goons stepped out.

"Damn it," I muttered, sizing him up. He was one of the bigger guys. Not quite as tall as Connor, but broader. And not in a nice way. He looked like a dump truck. Big and slow.

But I bet he hit *real* hard.

"What's wrong?" Connor murmured, his stance suddenly alert.

"This isn't one of the normal guards."

"Sora the Broken." The goon's voice rumbled with way too much bass, and I winced at the name. Not many people called me by it, but anyone who did was guaranteed to be an asshole.

"What'd you say?" Connor demanded. His tone was suddenly colder than I'd ever heard it, an implicit threat made a shudder run down my spine.

I shot him an appreciative glance. When I'd first met him, he'd looked like a guy who could handle himself in a fight. But he'd just transformed into someone who would win the fight without breaking a sweat. He'd probably do it with just his little finger.

Everything about him was coiled tension and the promise of deadly force. He might spend most of his time making delicate concoctions with his big hands, but I'd just figured out how he'd gotten all those scars on them.

Connor was used to fighting. *Very* used to it.

The guard scowled and ambled up to him. Connor stepped closer, his form radiating *threat*. It was a subtle thing—not the peacocking that the other guy was doing, sticking his chest out and trying to get a tiny bit of extra height.

No. Connor looked almost disappointed in his opponent. Disappointed but ready. It was the feeling in the air around him that made him scary. It prickled with latent violence. I desperately wanted to ask him to teach me how to do that.

The Devil's goon—Tommy, I thought his name was—shrunk back the tiniest bit and turned to me.

"What are you doing back here?" he hissed. "You got the stuff? Because you better have the stuff."

"Not yet. But I will."

"What do you mean, *you will*? The agreement was that you'd leave and get the potion. I'm here to make sure you don't try to sneak back in."

"Sneak back in?" I looked around. "I'm going through one of the main gates. This isn't *sneaking*."

"I don't know, you looked shifty."

That was a fair point. I often looked shifty since I was often up to no good. Connor, though.... I pointed to my companion. "Does he look shifty?"

The guard flicked him a glance, and the slightest bit of fear crept into his eyes.

A lot of the Devil's goons weren't so bad, but he did have some losers in the bunch. Tommy was definitely one of them.

Tommy turned back to me. "Why are you here?"

"Keep a civil tone in your mouth," Connor said, his voice icy.

Tommy paled slightly.

"Now try again," Connor said.

I preened. I could handle myself and was proud of it. But I'd be lying if I said I didn't like having someone to stick up for me. Two was always more powerful than one, and as someone with wonky magic who lived at the outskirts of magical society *because* of said wonky magic,

I quite liked having some power. And someone at my back.

"Why are you here?" Tommy asked again, much more politely this time.

"We need to get a potion ingredient from the witches so that we can make more of the Expulsio potion for the Devil."

He grumbled.

Connor gave him another cold look, and he backed up slightly. "Fine, fine. But I'm watching you."

"Whatever, Tommy." I gestured to the big gate. "Now let us in."

He sighed and turned. "Follow me."

We followed him to the small door, which led to a narrow, arched tunnel through the gatehouse. It was dark and cold inside, but Guild City beckoned at the other end, bathed in cool gray light.

Connor stayed close behind me, as if to guard my back, and we stepped out into the city.

The Devil of Darkvale didn't run the city—the Council of Guilds did that—but he did control some of the gates in the same way that the mob controlled certain neighborhoods back in the human world.

The Devil's goon melted into the shadows at the base of the wall that surrounded the city. In front of us, one of the small town squares opened up. Each of the gates had a courtyard in front of it, with shops surrounding the open space. The guild towers were like that as well, and they formed tiny neighborhoods within Guild City.

I tried to see it through Connor's eyes and thought it held up quite nicely. A lot of the architecture was medieval, two-story buildings of dark wood and white plaster. A few were painted colorful shades that added some cheer through the fog, and flowers tumbled from window boxes despite the cold. Mullioned windows gleamed dully under the pale light. The fog was particularly thick this morning, adding a really moody feel to the place. Gas lamps flickered, making it feel slightly haunted.

Despite the old style of the architecture, the shop windows were full of modern magical items. You could buy anything you wanted in Guild City. There was no end to the magic in this place.

"What do you think?" I asked.

"Charming." Connor looked around, his gaze moving from shop window to shop window. "Lots of stores."

"Guild City is known for its shopping, both the normal kind and the sort where you can go to a guild and make an expensive—and possibly dangerous—deal to hire their services."

"What do you mean?"

"Each guild specializes in something. Witches sell potions, sorcerers sell spells, seers sell visions, shifters provide protections services."

"Like bodyguards?"

"Or mercenaries. There are more guilds, too, each specializing in something different. They're the real draw to Guild City. But don't ignore the stores. They're pretty great." I pointed to a clothing shop. "Everything in there is enchanted. Want to be hotter? Buy from them. Or stronger?" I eyed him up and down. "Well, maybe you don't need that. But if you did, you could get a jacket that would let you lift a truck. Pants that would make you run like an Olympian, or a pair of fake wings that will take you to the clouds."

Something flickered in his eyes, but it was gone in a flash as he raised his brows and said, "Impressive."

I pointed to another store. The window was full of random stuff like brooms and pens and notebooks and toys. "That place sells weapons."

"Doesn't look like it."

I grinned at him. "It's sneaky like that. You can get boring old swords and knives at a place on the other side of town. That place turns everything normal into a weapon."

"Like James Bond, with his exploding pens."

"Yeah, but magical." I grabbed his hand for the hell of it and pulled him along. "Come on. I'll give you a better tour later."

He squeezed my hand tightly and didn't let go, and a frisson of delight traveled up my arm. This kind of flirting was unusual for me, but what could I say?

He inspired me.

And maybe it was also the fact that the Devil had my name on his Shit List. It made me feel like I had limited time left, and I was determined to live it up.

We passed one of the weirder bars in town, a vampire club that specialized in blood cocktails. As I preferred the normal stuff—bourbon, especially—it wasn't for me. Anyone could drink a blood cocktail, but only vampires really liked them.

The streets grew narrower as we cut deeper into the city, the buildings looming overhead. They were only two stories tall—three stories, in rare cases—but this street was so narrow that they seemed taller. The bottom levels were dedicated to more shops and bars, with apartments over the top.

"I live on a street just like this," I said, finding myself wanting to share something of my life with him.

"Do you like it?"

"Yeah." Something in his tone made me really think about it. *Did* I like it? Really and truly? "Mostly."

"What do you mean, mostly?"

"This is my home." I gestured around. "A totally magical city. What's not to love?"

"Magic's Bend is totally magic as well."

"Fair enough."

"You have to like more than the magic to really like it."

"I do." Except, if I really thought about it, it was a bit lonely. My wonky magic separated me from people. Everyone here knew that I had no control and could get them into the kind of trouble I'd been in earlier. Namely, naked by my own hand and unconscious.

It was hard to make friends like that.

But when the Devil of Darkvale had threatened to take this place away from me, I'd freaked.

Why?

Because it was the only home I'd ever known. Of course I didn't want to be booted out. But if given a choice...

Maybe this place wasn't the be-all end-all. I shook the thought away.

Nah. This place was amazing.

"We're headed to the other side of town," I said. "Each of the guilds owns a tower that is built into the city wall. Most of them aren't gates like the one we just passed through, but they are responsible for the defense of the city."

"Defense?"

"It was more important back in the day, when this place was built." I shrugged. "Now, the guilds form the government and make the rules. If we were ever attacked by a crazy person, they would mount the defense."

"Who lives in the towers?"

"The most important members of the guilds, but everyone needs to be a member of a guild. Because I'm a Void Mage, I belong to the Mages' Guild."

"But you don't live there."

I laughed. With my wonky magic? "Hell, no."

"Don't want to?"

"Once, I wanted nothing more. Now? No. Not for me."

"Why? Not a joiner?"

I had a feeling that I might actually be a joiner, if I could make some friends. That choice had been taken from me when my control over my magic had been stolen. But I decided to go with a lie. "Pretty much."

He shot me a skeptical look.

He *totally* didn't believe me.

But we'd arrived at the Witches' Guild. I withdrew my hand from his and pointed across the small clearing to the tower that was set into the huge wall surrounding the city. This clearing was grassier than the others, and the shops were more derelict.

I blamed it on the witches. They were so loud—and occasionally, destructive—that shops didn't want to open up near them. Little things would happen, like spells shooting from the chimneys and magical fires blazing across the lawn, that made it hazardous to be too close to their guild tower. The Council of Guilds was supposed to control them, but no one had quite managed it.

"Creepy," Connor said.

"Very." The witches' tower looked exactly like it should: a pale brown square building that leaned slightly to the left, topped with a dark, pointed roof that was vaguely reminiscent of a witch's hat. A wooden staircase wrapped around the sides, leading upward, and the windows were shadowed and eerily empty. Like a sociopath's eyes.

Pale blue smoke wafted from one of the chimneys, but it was the green smoke curling around the base of the tower that caught my eye. I took a tentative step toward the path that led up to the front door. The smoke curled away from the house and drifted toward us.

"Shit." I scowled at it.

"Not very inviting," Connor said.

"No kidding." The smoke was curling toward us along

the ground, creeping like an ephemeral snake with murder in its eyes.

"Is it normally there?"

"Not if you're invited."

"We don't have an invitation?"

"We should." Coraline was fucking with me. Damn it. "We'll be fine. Just be alert."

Carefully, I strode down the path, being sure to stick to the stone walkway. No way would I step on their grass. Connor kept close to my side, his stance once again alert. A faint mist smoked in the air, filling my head and making my thoughts slightly woozy.

"It's a hallucinogen," I said. "Sort of. It's meant to raise your anxiety level. Get you to think about things you're afraid of."

"Like Phantoms."

"I think it's distilled from their essence, yes. Try to ignore it." But it was hard. I could already feel my mind starting to twist, digging for the things that scared me.

I'm all alone.

I'll always be alone.

Guild City was my home, but there was no one here for me. And there never would be.

It isn't really my home.

Tears pricked my eyes, and I desperately wanted to suck in a bracing breath. Anything to clear my head. But I couldn't. That would just draw more of the horrible stuff into my lungs.

Connor reached for my hand and gripped it tight. I

looked at him, wondering what was going through his mind. His brow was creased and his eyes shadowed, but it was impossible to get a hint of what was happening inside his head.

"What's the thicker stuff near the ground?" He pointed to one of the thick green curls of smoke that crept toward us.

"More dangerous." As soon as I said it, the plume lurched off the ground and struck out for us, lunging like a massive snake.

Connor grabbed my waist and swung me around, diving to the side to avoid the thick smoke. He twisted in the air and landed hard on the grass, protecting me from the ground. I slammed onto him, his muscular body breaking my fall.

Quickly, he rolled over, pinning me beneath him and shielding me from whatever might attack from above.

Nothing more struck at us, the smoke having dissipated when it didn't hit us. The threat was gone.

Suddenly, all I could feel was Connor's strong form surrounding me. He leaned over me, both elbows propped on the ground near my head. He was so big, seeming to block out the light, and his evergreen scent wrapped around me.

All of the sad thoughts flew from my head, and there was only Connor. My gaze caught his. Tension tightened the air between us, and our surroundings disappeared.

Every breath he drew in made his chest swell, pressing it closer to mine. From here, I could see all the shades of green in his eyes. The heat in their depths mimicked the inferno that was blazing through me.

Somehow, I managed to force some reasonable words through my throat. "This is probably just an illusion. Magic."

"How I feel for you isn't an illusion." Connor's voice was rough. "And the mist causes anxiety. Not…this."

He was right. And the horrible thoughts that had been racing through my head had been replaced with thoughts of Connor. How much I wanted to spend time with him. Talk to him. Kiss him.

My gaze moved to his lips, which looked full and soft. Impossibly perfect. Perfectly kissable.

"Sora." His voice was soft. "If you look at me like that…"

Unable to help myself, I leaned up and kissed him, pressing my lips to his. He groaned low in his throat, his mouth moving on mine like this was the last kiss he'd ever have. I gripped the back of his neck as my head spun.

A cheer sounded in the distance, and I jerked back, tearing my lips from his.

He stiffened, his posture immediately returning to protectiveness. Quickly, he rolled to his feet and pulled me up. My lips were still vibrating as I rose, my senses on high alert.

The cheer had come from one of the upper windows of the tower, where I spotted a twitching curtain.

"Those bitches," I muttered.

"What's going on?"

"They were spying."

"Spying?"

"You'll see." I gripped his hand and pulled him forward. "Come on."

We walked toward the tower. Now that the witches were aware of our arrival, the protective mist had dissipated. The memory of it lingered, however, along with visions of Connor skillfully maneuvering me away from the threat.

"You're good at protecting people," I said.

"Not everyone," he replied, the slightest hint of bitterness to his voice. So minor I almost didn't hear it. He seemed to shake himself, as if realizing what he'd said. Smoothly, he turned to me. "Good enough at protecting you, though."

There was something genuine to his voice—satisfaction or something—that I liked. But I couldn't help but wonder who he hadn't protected in the past.

Another girl?

I hoped he didn't have some tragic history. I wanted whatever this was to work between us, and the ghost of a lost love was one quick way to screw that up.

5

Connor

As we walked up to the door, I counted my lucky stars that she hadn't asked who I'd failed to protect. It seemed to hang in the air between us, but I was glad we weren't discussing it now.

Guilt tugged at me, though.

She might think it was another girl.

And it *was* a girl, but...

Not how she was thinking. I'd failed to protect my sister. Our Fae court had evicted her, and I could do nothing to stop them.

I shook away the dark thoughts. That had been in a distant past, and Claire was fine now. *I* was fine now. And I'd be even better if I could help Sora get this Devil guy off her back.

Sora stopped in front of the narrow wooden staircase built along the side of the building. It started on one side and wound around to the other. She looked at me. "Ready?"

"Yeah. They're just some witches, right?"

"Sure." She winked at me.

I gestured to the building. "This place is pretty small, though. How many can there be?"

"It's bigger on the inside. And there are probably thirty, but we won't meet all of them."

I felt my brows rise. "Thirty?"

"Imagine a magical sorority house, but they can kill you." She grinned. "In fact, they'd be delighted to."

"Gotcha."

Together, we climbed the stairs. I could feel the prickle of magic that indicated a protection charm, but it wasn't active.

As if she could read my thoughts, Sora said, "They protect the front yard, but once you've made it this far, they aren't keen to stop people from approaching. They sell their spells and small charms, after all. It's their main source of income, so they don't want to drive off customers."

"And that green misty snake thing wasn't meant to drive off customers?"

"That was specially made for me, I think. They knew I'd power through."

"Friends of yours?"

She hesitated. "Undetermined."

"Normally, you know when people are your friends."

"Yeah, well...." She stopped in front of the small wooden door. "We're here."

She raised a hand and knocked, and we waited in silence. A few moments later, the door swung open, and a ghostly butler stood in front of us. His form flickered an ephemeral blue, and he was able to hold on to the door, which was unusual for ghosts.

He was dressed like an old-timey butler, with a starched black suit and high pointed collar. His brow seemed permanently raised halfway up his forehead, as if he were perpetually surprised or disapproving.

From the wrinkle of his nose, I had to guess it was disapproval.

"Jeeves," Sora said, her tone pleasant.

The butler nodded and stepped back to allow us to enter.

I leaned down and murmured into her ear. "Jeeves? You aren't serious, are you?"

"As the grave." She cracked a grin. "Where do you think the name originally came from, anyway?"

"Fair enough." I followed her into the dark foyer.

The space was small and covered with black velvet wallpaper. Underfoot, the wooden floor creaked ominously, like the floorboards would give away any minute and drop us down into a dungeon cellar. The scent of herbs and candles lingered in the air, along with something strangely sweet, but not unpleasant. It reminded me of the Apothecary's Jungle, a creepy shop-slash-house owned by my friends, Blood Sorceresses Aerdeca and Mordaca.

Except for the paintings on the wall. Those were done in bright shades of neon, making the subjects—wizards and witches in traditional garb—appear to be partying at a rave. And the lights in the chandelier—those were a bit weird as well. The bulbs were all colors of the rainbow.

The effect was kind of… insane.

A shrieking laugh echoed from the back of the house, followed by a scream that sounded something like, "I will murder you…stealing my pigeon, you…"

I shot Jeeves a look. "Her pigeon?"

"I really couldn't say, sir." He gestured to a small door in front of me. "Come, follow me."

Sora and I shared a look, then followed Jeeves into a small corridor. It struck me that I hadn't sensed any magic. Though it was clearly here—there was the unmistakable buzz of it—I got no hint of the dozens of magical signatures that should be shooting around this place if there were thirty witches present. Each of them would have at least one signature, but I could sense none.

Just like I couldn't sense it from Sora.

This town really was serious about keeping their magical signatures on the down-low.

Jeeves led us into a slightly larger room. The space was cluttered with four suits of armor, one in each corner. In the middle of the room sat two small, ornate couches facing each other. The electric lights had been replaced with open-flame candles—a serious fire hazard—and there were empty wine glasses scattered around on the little tables.

Jeeves's eyes went immediately to the glassware, and he made an annoyed *tsk*ing sound. I could almost feel his desire to mutter something, but he bit it back. That had to be a good butler trait, especially in a place like this. Not that I had much experience.

"Please, take a seat." Jeeves gestured elegantly to the chairs. "I will announce your presence, and someone will be with you shortly."

"Thanks, Jeeves," Sora said.

Together, we sat on the same couch. It was so small that my thigh pressed to hers, and the heat soaked through my jeans to my skin.

Screams and crashes echoed from the back of the building, and I looked at Sora. "So this is normal, right?"

"Oh, very." She nodded. "They're...kind of nuts."

"Cool. But they'll give us the ingredient?"

"Sell it to us, more like."

"Fair enough."

She leaned up to whisper in my ear, her words so soft that I could barely hear them. "We could be under surveillance, so let's keep details minimal."

I nodded.

The door banged open. Three witches tumbled in, and...

Well, yeah.

They were nuts.

The woman in the lead was young—not much over

twenty. She was tall and slender. Her jet black eyes gleamed with cunning under the candlelight, and neon green striped through her straight ebony hair. She was dressed like a ballerina, with a matching neon green tutu and tank top. The only difference was her extremely chunky black boots. She carried an enormous purse over one shoulder.

"That's Coraline," Sora whispered.

Behind her was a ghostly pale girl whose bright pink hair matched her eyes. She looked like an albino Easter rabbit, but she was dressed like a cowboy, with the chaps and everything.

I looked at Sora to get her name, and she murmured, "Mary."

The last girl to enter was slight but strong looking, with warm brown skin and blindingly white teeth. She was the only one dressed like a normal person in a T-shirt and jeans—that is, if you ignored the pigeon sitting on her shoulder and the green braids that had tiny black eyes at each tip.

At first glance, they looked like snakes. They weren't—just a very clever decoration—but the effect was eerie.

"That's Beth," Sora said.

Beth caught me looking at her hair and glared. "Medusa was misunderstood."

I'd had a friend run into the real Medusa once and share the story. "I agree."

The girl arched an eye, her tone challenging. "Met her?"

"No, but a buddy of mine has."

She shot me an impressed look.

"Are you having a costume party?" I asked.

"No." Coraline tilted her head and glared at me. "Why would you think that?"

"He's not from around here," Sora said. "Thank you for meeting us, though."

"Where's he from?" Mary looked me up and down, her lips pursed appreciatively. Made me feel a bit like a horse up for auction, actually. I wasn't a fan.

"Magic's Bend." I stood and held out my hand. "I'm Connor."

"Alchemist," Sora added.

"Potions Master," I corrected.

"Master, eh?" Mary grinned. "Must be good with your hands."

"Okay, okay, back off," Sora said. "Do you have the ingredient or not?"

"Calm down, calm down!" Coraline raised her hands in a placating gesture.

The three piled onto the couch and leaned forward, staring at us.

"So, you need the Ascencia root," Beth said.

"Powdered," I specified.

All three gave us sympathetic frowns.

"Well, that might be a bit hard," Mary said. "All we've got are seeds."

"You said you had it," Sora said, her tone irritated.

"And we do." Coraline shrugged. "You just need to wait for it."

"I don't have time to wait for it."

"The sorcerers have a spell that will make it grow fast," Mary said.

Beth elbowed her. "She can't ask the sorcerers."

"Right." Mary shrugged, clearly not caring. "You could break in, I guess."

Sora cursed.

"Anyway," Coraline said. "We need payment for the seeds."

"What have you got?" Mary's gaze moved between the two of us.

"Ah…" Sara's voice trailed off.

Before I could say anything, Beth leaned forward. "I know what we want."

"What?" Sora frowned.

"Your obsidian dagger. The enchanted one."

"No." Sora's voice was firm, but there was the smallest hint of fear at the edge of it.

Or maybe I was imagining that.

All three girls leaned forward, their eyes ravenous. They spoke in unison. "We want it."

Okay, maybe I hadn't imagined it. There was something going on here. I looked at Sora, spotting a sad cast to her eyes.

"Fine." She bit out the words, pulling a tiny dagger from her pocket. As she withdrew it, the thing lengthened in front of my eyes, growing into a wicked eight-inch blade.

The three witches all grinned, their eyes gleaming with greed.

I glanced back at Sora.

Yeah, she was sad.

This blade was special to her for some reason. It wasn't just that it was badass. I could almost feel her grief over parting with it. A gift from someone she loved? A parent, maybe? Boyfriend?

"You guys suck, you know," she said.

"Whatever." Mary grinned and held out her hands, her pink-tipped nails gleaming in the light as she made a grabby-hands gesture. "Give it over."

"Show me the seeds first," Sora said.

Beth's lips twisted in an unsurprised smile as she reached into her pocket and pulled out a tiny velvet bag. She poured the contents into her hand and held out the seeds for our inspection.

Sora looked between me and the seeds. "Well?"

Though they were tiny, each had the distinctive blue and red star pattern. I nodded. "They're the real deal."

"Told you." Mary smirked.

"Fine." Sora expertly flipped her dagger so that the hilt pointed toward the witches, then thrust it toward them. Coraline took it with a triumphant smile and slipped it into her huge bag, patting the side with a satisfied look.

Sora's eyes followed the dagger, and my heart ached for her.

Beth dumped the seeds back into the little bag and held it out to Sora. "Nice doing business with you."

"Sure." Sara's tone was sharp, and I was sure that if it hadn't been a matter of life or death—or at the very least, losing her home—she wouldn't have traded the dagger.

The witches laughed victoriously.

Sora stood and looked at me.

I nodded and rose, turning so that the witches couldn't see my hands as I withdrew a tiny vial from the sheath at my wrist. It was no bigger than an inch long, and the glass was so delicate that it would give a Christmas ornament a run for its money.

Sora turned and went to the door, and I followed. As I walked by the witches, I pinched the tiny vial in my hand, hoping my new potion would work. I'd tested it plenty, but never on witches. And it was impossible to know what kind of charms protected them or this place.

As the glass shattered between my fingers, a tiny cloud of pink dust exploded from my hand, and I looked at the witches.

The dust spread quickly. As soon as it touched each of the witches, they froze, time stopping around them. I was immune, thanks to the fact that I'd slowly built up a tolerance, but their bodies were completely susceptible.

They weren't dead, or even unconscious. Not technically, at least. They just had no idea what was going on around them.

As I wanted it to be.

Sora was far enough away that the dust couldn't reach her. She turned back to me. "You coming?"

I ginned at her.

Confusion gleamed in her eyes as she tilted her head and inspected the three witches, each of whom was still sitting on the couch in mid-laugh. "What did you do to them?"

"A new potion. Powder, actually. They have no idea that time has stopped, and when it starts back up again, they'll remember nothing."

"Why?"

I bent and hovered my hand over the bag into which Coraline had dropped the dagger. It sparked with protective magic, as I'd guessed. As I drew my potion bag from the ether, I asked Sora, "Do you want your dagger back?"

"Yeah. But..." She frowned. "They'll notice. And they'll want payment. I don't want the Witches' Guild after me."

"I thought you had friends here."

"Sort of? Not the kind who would let me steal from them, though."

"We'll leave something of greater value than the seeds." My gaze flicked to her. "The Ascencia seeds are valuable, but not *that* valuable. They just knew you were desperate."

"That's the truth. I *am* desperate."

"Not for long." I retrieved a potion from my bag that would temporarily disarm the charm on the bag and poured a drop onto the handles. The charm fizzed and broke, and I reached in to retrieve the dagger. I held it up. "What does this do?"

"Just what you saw. Turn really small and big on command. And it's a good-looking dagger."

She wasn't wrong. It was a beautiful weapon. But it wasn't insanely valuable. "So they wanted it because you want it."

"And because it's gorgeous."

I nodded. "Then we'll give them something they'll want more."

"What?"

"Proprietary potions of mine. I rarely share them, but when they get a load of what these babies can do, they'll be satisfied." I tucked the dagger under one arm and collected a half dozen of the most valuable potion bombs from my bag. My potions were unlabeled—I could tell what they were by color and shape of the glass container.

"Are you sure?" she asked.

"Of course. They didn't wait to see what I had to offer in a trade. And you were handing that dagger off so fast I'd think you didn't want it."

"I do." She scowled. "But that's not what you're here for. You're helping me make the potion. Not helping me with other stuff."

"Maybe I want to." As the words left my lips, I knew they were true. Except, it was a seriously loaded statement, and it hung heavy in the air. Every second that passed made me more confident that she was *the one*. Hell, I knew it.

I could freaking feel it.

She was my fated mate, and every ignored Fae bone in my body recognized it.

But Sora might not recognize it. And now was not the time to talk about it. And we needed to get out of here.

My gaze fell on a notebook and paper sitting on a table near the door. I jerked my chin toward it. "Will you get that for me, please?"

"Sure." She grabbed it and hurried over.

Quickly, I slipped the six potion bombs into the purse, then traded Sora for the notebook, giving her the dagger in exchange. I looked down at the notebook and spotted a crude drawing of two vampires going at it.

Oookay.

I flipped to a clean page and put pen to paper.

"What are you writing?" Sora asked.

"A description of each potion bomb and a note to find me for more if they want them. I'll make them a second batch free of charge if they leave you alone."

There was a moment of silence, and I realized that I was basically spilling my heart out to her. This was a *lot* of magical firepower I was trading on her behalf, and it wouldn't be cheap to make.

Whatever.

I finished the note and slipped it into Coraline's bag. "Okay, I'm going to snap them out of it. Go back to the door where you were so everything looks normal."

She nodded and shoved her dagger into her pocket, then turned and hightailed it to the door. I got into the same position I'd been in when I'd released the first potion and drew a second from my wrist cuff. This one was a pale green, and when I crushed the glass vial between my fingertips, a pale green mist escaped. A moment later, the witches immediately jerked back into action.

My heart pounded in my ears in the split second it took to see if they realized something was off, but they just keep laughing.

I strode quick to the door and followed Sora out into the hall. We didn't wait for Jeeves, just hightailed it toward the exit.

"Hurry," Sora whispered. "We need to get out of here before they go for the dagger. They'll strike before they read your note, I bet."

"That quick to violence, huh?"

"Oh, you don't know the Witches' Guild."

6

Sora

The witches' laughter echoed as I hurried through the foyer and out the main door. Watery sunlight gleamed as I took the stairs two at a time. Exhilaration surged through me.

I looked over my shoulder at Connor and said, "We totally pulled a fast one on the witches."

He grinned, his long legs eating up the ground as he followed me down the stairs. As soon as we reached the bottom, we broke into a run down the path. My heart pounded, and joy made me feel like I was floating.

As we sprinted toward the shelter of the streets, I began to laugh. "That was amazing."

"Those witches were bitches."

"Kinda." Laughing, I stumbled to a halt in the nearest alley, the narrow space providing a shadowed spot to hide.

Connor stopped next to me, and we turned back to the tower to look at it. The Witches' Guild tower still tilted ominously to one side, looking extremely creepy through the thin fog.

My laughter faded, and I turned to look at Connor. "Thank you for the help. Seriously."

"Anytime." His grin faded, replaced with a worried smile. "Those are your friends?"

"Not really."

"But you want them to be."

"Not really."

"Then what's up? There's something...wistful about you."

Could I tell him that I just wanted friends... like, full stop? That seemed really pathetic to admit. I was in my mid-twenties. I should have a ton of friends by now.

My silence must have lasted too long, because Connor changed track. "Why did the guard call you Sora the Broken?"

I hissed at the name. I'd mostly gotten people to stop calling me that. It'd been easier to hurl it at me when I was a teenager and couldn't hurl my obsidian dagger right back at them.

"And why have you been stealing so much from the Sorcerers' Guild?"

"*Attempted* stealing." I winked, knowing it probably

wasn't covering up my discomfort. "There's a much shorter jail time for that."

"Yeah, well, why?"

I bristled under the question. I didn't want to answer this. I hardly knew him. Why would I spill my guts to him about my sad sack of a life story? I much preferred to present the world with who I wanted to be, not who I was.

And the genuine caring in his eyes made me feel panicky. I wasn't used to this kind of thing.

I swallowed hard, mind racing. "Why should I tell you anything when you have your own secrets?"

"Because your secrets are the reason we're here."

I shrugged, not caring that it was true. "Whatever. If you want me to tell you my serious shit, you have to tell me yours. You've got a past…I can see it. There's conflict floating around you like an aura."

His jaw firmed, and his eyes flashed dark.

Clearly, he was debating.

"Come on. You show me yours, and I'll show you mine," I said.

His eyes sparked with a different kind of darkness, and I found that I liked it. I punched him lightly in the arm, just to keep him on track. "Come on, spill."

He leaned against the alley wall and looked in both directions, as if checking to see whether other people were around. Or he was stalling. Either way, I was surprised when he finally opened his mouth.

"I'm Fae."

My brows rose. "I couldn't tell."

He tapped his rounded ears. "Hidden."

"Wings?"

"Gone."

"Gone?" I frowned. "That's possible?"

He nodded. "Definitely."

"That's terrible. How did it happen?" He *could* understand what my life felt like. He'd had his magic taken from him as well.

His gaze cut to mine, and there was something I couldn't read in it. "I chose it."

"What?" Surprise flashed through me. "Why would you ever do that?"

"You sure you want to hear this whole thing?"

"More than ever. Because I've no idea why you'd *ever* give up your magic."

"For my sister."

"Ah." Understanding dawned. "The one you couldn't protect."

He nodded. "She's not dead or anything, thank fates. My story doesn't take quite that tragic a turn. But when we were teenagers in the Fire Fae Court, it was prophesied that she would be the fated mate of a rival king who would kill her. *And* she was fated to be the savior of our people, though no one knew how."

"Hoo boy, that's some kind of burden."

"No kidding. Especially when you're basically a kid and your court evicts you to *save* you. Or so they say."

"They really did that?"

"Yes. As long as she stayed in our court, the King of the

Sea Fae could find her. And our own king and queen had the terrible idea to bind her magic so that she could hide in the real world."

"But they basically just kicked you guys out."

"Just her. They were going to kick her out alone and expect her to hide until the day came when it was time for her to go home and save them all." He gave a bitter chuckle and dragged his hand through his hair. "They knew her well enough to know that she *would* do it, too. Claire is nothing if not honorable."

"Claire isn't a very Fae name." She frowned. "For that matter, Connor isn't, either."

"Not our real names." A small smile twisted his lips. "After I gave up my wings and ears to hide with her, we took human names. Back home, she's Caera, though she doesn't go by that name."

"And you?"

"I was Caspian."

"But you don't go by it anymore."

"No. And I never will again."

"So what happened to your sister?"

"She's fine now. Happily married to the same Sea Fae who was going to kill her."

I raised my eyebrows. "Sounds like a story."

"It is. And she has her wings back. She needed them to fulfill her destiny and save our people."

"But the king and queen never gave you your wings back?" Indignation surged through me.

"They offered, but I didn't take them up on it."

"Why the hell not, if your sister had them back? Was it a loyalty thing? You didn't want anything from them because they were horrible to your sister?"

"Playing armchair psychologist?"

"Maybe. Am I wrong?"

He shrugged, and I felt there was more he wasn't saying. "Like I said, I didn't want them back." Absently, his hand went to his pocket. "And I created a potion years ago that would give me my wings back if I ever really wanted them."

"You did?" Shocked, my gaze moved to his pocket. "You've been carrying a cure around all this time and have never taken it?" I couldn't even imagine. My entire life had been about finding a cure for the curse on my magic, and this guy had one in his pocket all along and wouldn't even take it. Annoyance spiked. "Hell, Connor. I appreciate your loyalty, but this is too much."

His lips twisted. "It's not just loyalty, Sora. Don't go thinking I'm some hero that I'm not."

"What do you mean?"

"It's easy to give up magic. Deadly to try to get it back." He pulled the tiny vial out of his pocket and held it up. "I carry this because I feel compelled to. But the minute I take it, I start a deadly transition that I may or may not survive."

"Then why the hell didn't you just take your wings when the king and queen offered them?"

"They don't actually have the power to give them back, even though I let them think that." He shoved the vial back in his pocket and rubbed his shoulder absently, as if he were missing his lost appendages. "My wings were more than just wings. They contained rare magic. When I gave them up, I gave up that magic. The king and queen couldn't give that back because they had no idea it existed."

Understanding dawned. "And that's why it's so hard to get your wings back."

"Precisely." He dragged a hand over his face. "And I keep having these dreams that once I get my power back, a village will burn."

"Which village?"

He shrugged, his eyes dark and sad. "I don't know. I don't even know if it really happens. It's just a vision I have."

"Maybe it doesn't happen."

"Maybe."

I wanted to ask him what the magic was, but he looked so tense that I thought he might break. He'd clearly shared as much as he was willing. I sighed and leaned against the wall. "That's some messed-up shit, dude."

He shrugged. "Not that bad. All my choice."

"That makes it weirder." I shot him a look. "Ever consider getting a therapist? I think you've got some stuff to work through."

He chuckled. "It's not the worst idea." His laughter faded. "But I've got a feeling that your damage wasn't your choice, was it?"

"So that's how it's going to be? Just going to change the subject to me, now?"

"I showed you mine."

He had. "And you know my problem is like yours. That I've got damage—except I didn't choose it."

"You wouldn't be called Sora the Broken otherwise."

I hissed, not liking the nickname.

"Sorry," he said. "If it helps, I don't think you're broken."

"I am." I shot him a guilty look. "I don't think I'm going to be able to pay you for your help like I said I would. That promise to void your opponents' weapons in battle? Yeah, not going to happen. Not unless you want to risk me voiding your side's weapons and also knocking you unconscious."

"Your void magic is screwed up."

I nodded. "I was cursed when I was a teenager. It was part of an ancient prophecy"—I scoffed bitterly—"something from a wizard who had a bone to pick with one of my ancestors, which is a load of bullshit, as far as I'm concerned. I'm a totally different person, but he cursed me anyway to fulfill the prophecy."

Connor glanced around, as if inspecting Guild City. "That kind of thing is normal here?"

I shrugged. "It's been an all-magical city for centuries. And I know that Magic's Bend is all magical, but it's a newer place. This city has been here more than five hundred years. That's a long time. There's a ton of history here, and not all of it good. The fairy tales weren't wrong when they told stories of ancient grudges carried down through generations."

"Do you know what your ancestor did to incur the wrath of this wizard?"

"No, and it doesn't matter. She didn't deserve it. And neither do I."

"I can definitely agree that you don't deserve it."

"Thank you." I nodded, getting pissed now, the way I did anytime I thought of my situation. "I used to have control, but after the wizard found me and cursed me... boom! Now I'm a disaster."

"And you've been trying to steal a cure."

"Nailed it in one go." My mind flicked back over my many attempts. "The sorcerers used to have it, but they wouldn't share."

"They don't have it anymore?"

"That's what I heard. They got rid of it to keep me from trying to break in. Not that it would have really worked, I found out. Stealing one of their spells is tricky because all of their spells must be performed *by* someone from their guild. They're not like the witches, who will sell you a potion to take on your merry way. They want more control."

"Because their spells are more dangerous?"

"Partly. And it's just how they work. Adds value to their services. Which I could never afford."

"What was the curse that the wizard placed on you?"

"The Curse of the Pereplet, from the distant reaches of Siberia."

"Sounds like a tough one to break."

"You're telling me." I clunked my head back against the stone wall. "But I'll get it one day." From my tilted-back position, I shot him a wry look. "I almost had it, too. That's why I was robbing the Devil. I found another wizard to break the curse, if I would bring him an Expulsio potion. In exchange, he'd do a spell to fix me."

"And now that's a moot point, because the Devil wants his potion back."

"Exactly. But I voided it into nowhere. And now I have to choose. I can either get evicted from Guild City or get my magic back. I choose home." I gestured at our surroundings.

He looked around, skeptical. "It's nice, but it's not home."

"It is."

"Do you have any friends or family here?"

"Well..." Shame burned me. Even though it shouldn't. It wasn't *my* fault that my magic had been broken by a bastard wizard, making me such a threat to all around me that they avoided me like the plague.

"That's what I thought." Connor gripped my shoulder. "Home has friends and family."

I opened my mouth to argue that I wasn't *so* pathetic that I didn't realize that—I had some buddies! Not that close, but I had them. But a figure appeared at the end of the alley, walking toward us. There was no threat from the person. Even from this distance, I could tell they weren't one of the Devil's people, but they were going to interrupt the conversation.

"Come on. Let's go." I left the alley and headed onto the main road. Connor joined me, and we walked quickly down the street. "The Sorcerers' Guild isn't far from here. We can get the growing spell and have those seeds turned into plants in no time."

Connor was silent as he walked alongside me, as if he were chewing over everything that I'd told him. Unease streaked through me—what did he think of me now?

Normally, I liked to carefully control how people saw me. But this...

I'd just laid it all out there, like a naked sunbather.

Only in this case, there were no boobs to distract him. Just the cold, hard truth of my screwed-up magic. And the fact that I couldn't pay him back for his help in the way that I'd promised. I shot him a glance out of the corner of my eye, grateful to see that he hadn't turned around and ditched me.

He was still going to help me.

Since he was silent as the dead, I had no idea *why* he was going to do it. But I wouldn't push my luck and ask. Not until the Devil was off my back.

Finally, we reached the clearing in front of the sorcerers' tower. It was a monstrosity of stone, looming out of the thick city wall that stretched on either side of it, wrapping around all the other buildings in town. The tower itself rose four stories over most of the other buildings. There were few windows breaking up the expanse of gray stone that made the façade, and the entire place radiated with threat.

Connor whistled low under this breath. "These guys have something to prove, don't they?"

I chuckled. "They take themselves seriously." That was one thing I liked about the witches. They were bitches, but they didn't take themselves seriously. And I'd had my good times with Beth, Coraline, and Mary, but they'd always been after my obsidian dagger. Maybe because they wanted it, maybe to fuck with me.

But it didn't matter.

I patted my pocket. I had it back.

The main door of the Sorcerers' Guild was a huge black thing with an arched top. Steel studs decorated it, making it look as ominous as I knew the inside of the building to be.

"Is there another entrance?" Connor asked, turning to inspect the buildings on the other side of the green that faced the sorcerers' tower. "Some of these bars and restaurants are open. If we try to break in the front door, people will notice."

He was right. This was one of the nicer parts of town, with chic restaurants and bars that filled up with the brunch crowd. It was now early afternoon, and the businesses were hopping.

"There's a door on the far side, kind of hidden." I pointed toward the narrow space against the city wall where I knew the door was nestled. There were big, shady trees there, concealing a door that was set back against the exterior wall of the city.

"That'll do." Connor started toward it, but I grabbed his arm.

"Hang on." I pulled him back, and he turned to look down at me. "Thank you."

He nodded. "Yeah. 'Course."

He said it like it was obvious he'd help me. But it really *wasn't* obvious. We barely knew each other. The attraction was off the charts, but that didn't change things. We barely knew each other.

I wasn't going to point that out. I needed his help too much, and he was willing to give it.

Together, we cut across the square toward the far side of the building. Connor grabbed my hand and pulled me close, leaning down to talk. "Pretend we're into each other and we're looking for a place to make out. In case anyone in the bars is looking."

"No problem." I could fake that easy, since I'd be a big fan of finding a place to make out with him. I leaned against him, stumbling slightly, as if I'd had too many mimosas. It'd be easier to sell this charade if it were eleven p.m., but with any luck, this would do the job.

Together, we stumbled to the side wall of the tower, and Connor pressed me against it, his form warm and hard against mine. He dipped his head to my neck as if he were kissing me, but his lips barely brushed my skin as he whispered near my ear. "Any tips on how to get through the door?"

A shiver raced over me at the feel of his words against my skin. "No. I used to use my lock picks, but they got rid of the lock after my second attempt."

"Okay. We'll figure something out."

The door was still a good twenty feet farther back, closer to the wall that surrounded the city. We needed to get back there, and I wanted to make it believable. So I raised my head until our faces were lined up with each other's, then pressed my lips to his.

Warmth rushed through me at the press of his mouth, and his scent wrapped around me like a hug. I wanted to breathe him in for hours, kissing him against this wall until we both melted into a puddle.

But we had to keep moving.

With a shove, I maneuvered him so that his back was against the wall, closer to the door. Ravenous, I clutched his shoulders and kissed him like I was starving.

He groaned low in his throat, and his strong hands gripped my waist.

"I know this is a charade to get me toward the door," he muttered against my mouth. "But I'd keep it going all night."

Heat flared, and I pulled him toward me, kissing him like I couldn't get enough. And it was the truth—I couldn't. I could kiss him for hours. Skillfully, he flipped me around so that I was pressed against the wall deeper in the shadows of the tree. By now, no one could see us, and I kissed him for all I was worth.

7

Connor

Sora's mouth moved on mine like she was ravenous for me, and the heat streaked through my veins like fire. I wanted to devour her, spending hours kissing every inch of her.

But now was not the time.

With a regretful groan, I pulled away from Sora. "We need to make our move before the sorcerers notice we're out here."

Panting, she leaned her head against the stone wall. "Good point. Let's get to it."

I moved toward the corner where the tower met the city wall. There was nothing but stone. "There's no door."

"Hidden." She pointed to the ground.

Everything looked normal except for the fact that the grass was a little more trampled. "I don't see it."

"Do you have a potion to reveal hidden things? I used to bring one when I'd come to break in."

"Yeah." This was one that I kept in a wrist cuff, and I pulled it free.

"Nice," Sora said. "That's how you froze the witches without us noticing?"

"Yeah. Subtlety can be useful." I unscrewed the tiny cap and poured a minuscule drop on the ground.

Immediately, the grass and earth disappeared, revealing stone steps leading down about ten feet to a small, sturdy wooden door.

"The sorcerers live underground," Sora said. "The tower is where they store their goodies."

I grimaced, not liking the idea of living underground. "Weirdos."

"Seriously."

She walked down to the door. I stashed the remainder of my potion back in my cuff and joined her on the lowest step. She pointed to the spot where a door handle should be. There was nothing but flat wooden door. "See? They got rid of the lock and handle. Thanks to me."

"You can break into anything, huh?"

"Anything that has a lock." She scowled. "Bastards."

"I've got this." I dug into my potions sack and withdrew a disintegration bomb.

"That will unlock the door?" she asked.

"No. I'm going to destroy it."

She grinned. "My kind of guy."

I found that I wouldn't mind being her guy. Hell, who was I kidding? I aggressively *wanted* to be her guy.

"Do I need to back up?" she asked.

"No, this one doesn't explode." I uncorked it and poured the potion all over the door. It hissed and sizzled, eating away at the wood and magic that kept us out of the tower. Within seconds, the door was gone.

Sora ginned. "Nice."

"I've got an invisibility potion, too. Let's take it."

She nodded. "You're prepared."

"Always." I drew two small vials from my bag and handed her one. "Once we've each drunk one, we'll be able to see each other, but no one will be able to see us."

I tossed mine back, ignoring the disgusting flavor. I was used to it by now.

She took hers and uncorked it, then swigged it back. A grimace twisted her features. "Gross. You ever think of adding some flavoring?"

"Like strawberry or something?"

"Like whiskey. Or rum." She shuddered. "That needs something powerful."

I grinned. "I'll take it under advisement."

"Now or never." She stepped through the door into a long, gleaming corridor. The walls, floor, and ceiling seemed to be made of shining black glass that gleamed with an impossible light, illuminating the hall in a way that made me feel like I was in outer space.

"This place is wild."

She shivered. "They're creepy."

"And you're glowing." I stared at her, feeling a frown twisting my features. "And sparkling."

"So are you. I can't really make out your face." She gestured to her own. "It's too…glittery."

"Yours, too." I touched the smooth glass wall, feeling the magic within. "Something in this building is interfering with the invisibility potion."

"At least no one can identify us like this."

She had a point. We might not be totally invisible, but no one could pick us out of a lineup since we sparkled like glitter bombs, so it was an improvement. "It'll have to do. Which way do we go?"

"Follow me." She started forward, and I stuck close by her side. "There might be different protections in place, but I know the basic directions."

Together, we moved silently and quickly down the hall, passing several other hallways. Each was identical to the first, endless expanses of black glass that threatened to make me lose my way.

"There are no doors," I murmured.

"None that you can see."

We reached a crossroads and stopped. Five other hallways joined ours, forming a star. Magic seemed to pulse from the space, reaching inside my head and twisting.

I blinked, feeling my thoughts slip sideways. "What's going on?"

"Um…" Sora frowned.

A strange thought slipped into my mind, taking root and growing like an oak. "We should find the sorcerers."

"You're right." She looked at me, eyes oddly bright. "I think I know where they are. We should tell them what we've done to the door."

"And what we planned to do in their tower of treasure." I nodded, the idea exploding inside my head. It felt... wrong, somehow. But I couldn't get rid of it. "We should definitely tell them we were going to steal from them."

Sora gripped my hand. "Come on, I know the way to them."

She pulled me, and I hurried to join her, hoping we could find the sorcerers soon and turn ourselves in. Something deep inside me shouted that this was a bad idea, but I ignored it. This was definitely a good idea.

"Hang on." Sora stopped, pulling hard on my arm. "We can't go to them."

"Yes, we should." *No!* Something inside me shouted. But it was easy to ignore. I pulled on Sora's hand. "Come on, let's find them."

"No." Sora squeezed my hand painfully tight. "We're enchanted."

I blinked, the words making sense. "Holy fates."

She nodded, then shook her head fiercely, as if trying to drive out the thoughts. I pinched my arm so hard it would bruise fiercely, but the pain steadied me. Using the few seconds of mental clarity, I drew a tiny potion from my wrist sheath and stepped close to Sora. I crushed the glass vial so that smoke rose up from it, and inhaled.

My head began to clear immediately.

"Breathe it in," I said.

She drew in a deep breath. "That feels better. I can think straight. Mostly."

"Which way to the tower? We need to power through."

"Come on." She pulled my hand hard, and we ran back to the crossroads. I held my breath as she turned left and ran. The sorcerers' enchantment was so strong that it was difficult to fight the pull of their magic, even with the help of the clarity smoke that we'd inhaled.

Together, we pulled each other along as the magic tried to force us to betray ourselves. Finally, we got far enough away from the crossroads that the strange effect seemed to fade.

We stopped, panting, and leaned against the wall.

"I hate shit like that," I muttered.

"Same. But come on. We're almost there." She moved slowly and silently down the hall, her form alert for any attack. At the end of the hall, the narrow space opened up to a larger room. Within, there was a massive emerald door guarded by two sorcerers in long sapphire robes.

"This is it," she said. "We need to keep one of them conscious to perform the spell that we steal from the tower."

"I've got just the thing. Can you distract them so that they're paying attention to you?" Shit, that could be dangerous. "Actually, what kind of long-range magic do they have?"

"They won't strike right away. Don't worry about me."

Still, I did.

She glared. "I mean it."

"Okay, okay."

"See you in a sec." She straightened and strode out into the main room.

The two sorcerers frowned at her, clearly confused by her glittering form. They could see her, but they didn't recognize her.

"Hey, boys." She spoke in a far lower tone of voice, and with any luck, they'd never know who she was.

They stepped away from their posts, and she walked toward the far side of the room, forcing them to turn toward her. If either turned his head, he'd be able to see me, but I just needed to get behind them enough to throw the cage bomb. I only had one, so I couldn't risk them seeing it and smacking it out of the air with a spell.

Sora kept up a running commentary about how hot they looked in their uniforms—which was hilarious, considering that they were essentially just capes that made the sorcerers look like sapphire pillars—but they seemed to buy it. Or else, they thought she was nuts.

Either way, their attention was distracted enough.

I pulled the proper potion bomb from my bag and sprinted out of the hall, running on silent feet to get behind the guards. One of them twitched but didn't turn, seemingly entranced by Sora's glittering form.

When I was in position, I chucked the potion bomb. It flew through the air and smashed to the ground behind them. Arcs of electric light shot upward and over them, forming a domed caged that trapped them—and their magic—inside.

They spun, their cloaks swirling, and their mouths opened on silent shouts. Magic sparked around them but couldn't escape the cage.

Sora hurried back to me. "The cage blocks sound?"

"It blocks everything." I turned to the door. "Come on."

We ran toward the huge emerald door, which shimmered with a pale green light as we approached.

"What's the deal with the door?" I asked.

"Don't know."

I reached it and hovered my hand over the handle. Protective magic sparked. Before I could reach for my potion bag, figures leapt from the door. Eight emerald green soldiers who gleamed like jewels converged on us. Their faces were entirely smooth, and they didn't look human. They didn't look like stone, either, and they moved with a grace that was eerie.

I jerked Sora backward, reaching into the ether for the sword that I kept stashed there. Sora plunged her hand into her pocket and withdrew the black blade. It lengthened into a sword.

Armed, we lined up back to back.

The emerald guards charged, and I struck out with my blade, slashing into one. My sword severed an arm, which dropped to the ground with a strange thud instead of shattering like I'd expected. No blood poured, and the creature kept moving. I struck out again, severing it in half at the waist. It tumbled into two pieces, then lay still on the ground.

Behind me, Sora fought her attackers with grace and

speed, her black blade whirling. The attackers swiped out with their arms, which had lengthened into green blades.

Adrenaline pumped through my veins as I attacked, slicing out with my sword as I ducked blows from the emerald army. Time flew as I hacked away at them, ducking and dodging their blows.

The guard in front of me raised a hand, which widened and broadened to form a gleaming green shield. My blade clanged off it, and I kicked up, smashing my boot into the shield and sending the guard flying backward. One by one, I took them out, leaving their prone bodies lying around me like strange, gleaming jewels.

When all of the guards were still, I turned to Sora, my breath heaving.

She looked at me, eyebrows raised. "Well done."

"You too."

"I took out one. You got the other seven."

"Yours was big."

"It wasn't. I'm just not much with a sword." She looked me up and down. "Whereas you are."

I shrugged. "Practice." I turned to the door. "Now, let's get this spell."

The heavy door opened easily, and we stepped into an enormous square room. It was probably a hundred feet wide in each direction, but it soared overhead, rising over two hundred feet straight up. Shelves surrounded us on all sides, and hundreds of tall ladders reached toward the ceiling twenty stories overhead, going from shelf to shelf like in an old-fashioned library. The shelves themselves were packed with millions of bottles of ingredients, fully made potions, and presumably spells—which were essentially potions that required extra magic and incantations to work.

"It's bigger inside than it looked on the outside," I said.

"Like the witches' tower. Most of the guilds are enchanted this way." She ran toward the side wall. "Come on. We need to check the map."

"The map?"

"Yeah. It'll show us where to find what we're looking for."

I joined her in the corner, where she stood over a massive book that sat on an ornately carved pedestal. She flipped through the pages, muttering to herself. Finally, she pointed to a page. "There!"

I leaned over her shoulder, spotting the growing spell that we sought. It was located about halfway up on the far wall, nestled on the right side.

An idea flared. "Give me a moment."

"What?" Surprise sounded in her voice.

"Go get the other ingredient, I need to find something."

"What do you mean, you need to find something?" There was the slightest strangeness to her voice, but we didn't have time to discuss it now. More guards would be coming any minute.

"Hurry, I'll catch up," I said.

She huffed, but turned and hurried to the shelves.

I flipped through the book, looking for a specific ingredient. It was a rare one—so rare I'd never even seen it before. But if they had it, I might be able to remove the curse that made it impossible for Sora to control her magic.

Finally, I found the page with the ingredient's name: *Rowenia bark*. A very rare type of rowan tree that had been extinct for ages, but the sorcerers had a bit of the bark preserved. It looked like it was at the very top of the tower, which made sense, since it was so valuable.

Armed with the info, I sprinted into the middle of the room. Sora was already partway up the wall, climbing quickly up the ladders like she was in some kind of video game.

I hurried to join her, scaling the wooden rungs as fast as I could. We didn't have long to spare, and it would take time to reach the very top

About fifty feet overhead, Sora stopped near a shelf.

"You got it?" I asked.

"I think so."

"Okay, I'm headed to the top for one more thing."

"It's too dangerous. Guards will be coming soon."

"It's worth it." I climbed fast, missing whatever she shouted at me. She was right about the guards. They had to have been alerted by us breaking into this room. No way eight magical emerald fighters could come to life without their sorcerer masters knowing about it.

My muscles burned as a I climbed, lungs heaving. An alarm began to sound, the shrieking noise tearing at my eardrums and making my head ache. My heartbeat pounded as I raced upward, determined to get what I needed to help Sora.

Finally, I reached the top and searched through the shelves, trying to find the chips of bark.

"Hurry!" Sora's voice hissed from below me, and I looked down.

She'd climbed up to join me, and was only about ten feet below my ladder.

"I'm coming!" Suddenly, I spotted the bark. It was contained in a little glass jar, which I grabbed and shoved in my pocket.

Shouts sounded from below, and I looked down just in time to spot two sorcerers run into the room. Their ruby cloaks flapped around their legs as they looked upward. One of them raised a hand and shot a blast of green magic at us.

It struck Sora, and she lost her grip on the ladder.

Her shriek iced the blood in my veins. She began to fall, and everything turned into slow motion. I could see her floating in the air as she started the two-hundred-foot fall toward the stone floor below.

"Sora!" My heart lurched into my throat.

There was no way she could grab one of the ladders, no way she could stop herself.

And I didn't have a potion that could save her.

Panic flared, and my mind raced, moving a million miles a minute.

There was only one way.

I didn't even think. The consequences of this action—

whether or not I would survive—didn't matter. I'd live long enough to save Sora.

If it worked.

Please work.

I yanked the potion from my pocket and popped the top off, then swigged it back. Prayers raced through my head as the magic shot through my veins.

Sora continued to fall, and fear nearly drove me out of my mind. Pain flared at my back, and my wings burst forth. It was an insane, heady feeling. Something I hadn't felt in years.

I launched myself off the ladder, not knowing if my wings would even work. Had they come back strong enough?

Didn't matter.

I had to try.

I shot downward, my wings pushing me hard. It took everything I had to control my movements, and I barely managed. I raced gravity, desperate to reach her before she hit the ground.

8

Sora

Wind tore past me as I plummeted, fear like I'd never known freezing my bones. Somehow, that sorcerer had hit me with a spell. Above me, Connor raced for me, his ebony wings flared wide.

In a clash of limbs, Connor collided with me, and we spun through the air. I clung to him, my arms and legs wrapped tight around his body. My heart threatened to beat its way out of my chest, and fear had turned my limbs into a shaking mess. It took all my strength to keep my grip on him.

The world spun around us, and my mind buzzed with panic. We were going so fast, and we were so close to the ground.

We might hit.

Connor's magic flared, and his wings moved powerfully. Finally, they caught the air and pushed us toward the ceiling.

"Oh fates, you got me." Shock flashed as I looked behind him. "With your wings. But you said getting them back was deadly."

"Don't worry about it."

"Are you kidding?"

Below us, the guards shouted. I looked down, spotting them as they started to hurl magic toward us. It exploded, flashes of green indicating a sonic boom that could knock us out of the air.

Fear made my heart thud, and I was distracted from his wings.

Connor darted right. "We can't let them hit us."

"Give me your bag of potion bombs."

He called on it, dragging it from the ether and shoving it between us. We were glued chest to chest, so I was able to dig around inside of it.

As I tried to find an appropriate bomb, Connor flew in circles to approach the ground, making sure to stay near the walls. The guards seemed unwilling to throw their blasts of magic toward the shelves of potions, so his technique kept us safe for now.

"What's this?" I pulled out a round blue one.

"A stunner. Use it." He reached into the bag for another one, pulling out a red star-shaped bomb.

I chucked my own bomb at the guards, hitting one

right in the chest. He tumbled backward and slammed to the ground, unconscious.

Connor landed near the other sorcerer, who was still on his feet. I untangled myself and jumped off him. The sorcerer raised his hand, his palm glowing with green light, but Connor was faster. He threw his potion bomb, hitting the sorcerer in the chest.

The guard didn't so much as twitch, and Connor lunged for the guy. He was nearly as tall as my Fae, but far thinner. Connor grabbed his arms and pulled them behind his back, holding him tight with one hand. With his other hand, he deftly removed a tiny vial from his wrist sheath.

"What's that?" I asked.

"It'll make him help us. The first bomb—the red one—has wiped his memory. He won't remember a thing about this." Connor's gaze flicked to me. "Did you get your spell?"

"Yeah." I yanked it out my pocket, worried about his wings. He'd said getting them back was deadly…

And why the hell had he gone to the top of the tower?

"Hold the spell out," Connor said.

I did as he asked, holding out the small glass globe that glowed with light. In my other hand, I held the seeds.

Connor directed his attention to the sorcerer. "We need you to make this spell work on these seeds so that they grow."

The sorcerer's gaze was blank as he nodded.

"Hang on," I said. "Will the seeds need dirt to grow?"

"Not with the spell." The sorcerer's voice echoed hollowly.

"Then get to work." Connor released the guy's hands and rested one of his own on his shoulder. "Quickly."

The sorcerer's dark brows drew together as he raised his hands over the seeds. Magic sparked from his palms as he met my gaze. "Open the vial."

I popped open the lid, and the pale wisps of golden magic floated out. The sorcerer began to chant words I'd never heard before. It was almost like he was singing to the smoke, and it followed his command the way a cobra would follow a snake charmer. The smoke curled around the seeds in my palm, surrounding them. They glowed, beginning to unfurl as a tiny green stalk shot from each seed.

As they grew, the alarms blared all around. More sorcerers would be here any minute. My heart raced as I watched the magic work. We were so close…

Within seconds, four beautiful flowers lay in my palm. I grinned. "It worked."

Connor released his grip on the sorcerer's shoulder. The guy just stood there, staring into space.

"Will he be all right?" I asked.

"Yes. He'll come back to himself in a few minutes. Let's get out of here." He turned and headed for the door, folding his wings back into his body.

I followed him, confusion ricocheting inside of me. He had grown his wings to save me. But why had he climbed to the top of the tower? What had he wanted?

Had he decided to take payment for my services from the sorcerers, stealing something for his potion business?

But he'd said getting the wings back was deadly. Was I really worth that to him?

With the alarm blaring and threats coming from all around, there was no time to ask. I raced after him, following him through the entry hall. The guards were still in their cage, shouting and cursing.

Connor hurried down the corridor, and I followed. We were nearly to the exit when four guards spilled out of the hall in front of us. Connor didn't even slow. He charged, colliding with them. He knocked one unconscious with a hard punch, then kicked another in the chest. That guard choked and slammed against the wall, drifting down.

One of the remaining two guards managed to land a punch to Connor's shoulder, but Connor didn't even slow. He just returned the favor, hitting the guy square in the nose.

I managed to grab the last one, slamming the hilt of my dagger down onto his head. He slumped to the ground, unconscious.

"Come on." Connor grabbed my hand, and we raced from the Sorcerers' Guild, sprinting through the tiny door that was now missing and running up the stairs.

As soon as we reached the grass, Connor dug into his pocket and pulled out a transport charm. He chucked it to the ground and dragged me inside. The ether sucked us in and spun us around, spitting us out in Magic's Bend, right in front of Connor's bar, Potions & Pastilles.

I gasped and stumbled against him.

He caught me, holding me steady. "Are you all right?"

"Fine." My gaze flicked up to his. We'd nearly been caught. I'd nearly died. He had his wings, which could apparently kill him somehow. Anger surged. "What was so important that you went rogue? If we'd just gone for the one ingredient, we wouldn't have run into so much trouble. You wouldn't have been forced to take the potion for your wings."

"It was worth it, I promise."

Memories of falling to my death flashed in my mind's eye. "You saved me."

He gripped my shoulders gently. "Of course I did."

I swallowed hard. "What does this mean for you and your wings? You said it was deadly."

He ignored the question and released one of my shoulders, then reached into his pocket, pulling out a small glass jar of bark. "This is Rowenia bark. It's an ingredient for the potion that will remove your curse."

Shock raced through me. "What?"

"When you described the curse, I knew I had a potion recipe that could remove it. But there was one ingredient I've never had access to. It's one reason your curse has been so hard to get rid of. Nearly impossible to get the supplies."

My gaze flashed between his face and the little glass jar. "But you found it? For me?"

"Of course." A smile tugged up at the corner of his mouth. "I wasn't going to let a golden opportunity like that pass me by."

I threw my arms around his neck and kissed him hard on the mouth, joy filling me.

He'd done that *for me.*

To help me.

He'd had my back. Like really, truly had my back. More than anyone ever had since my parents died.

I pulled back. "Thank you so much."

"Maybe save that until we see if I can really make the potion to remove the curse."

"Thank you anyway, even if it doesn't work." Tears pricked my eyes. "Knowing that you did that for me...well, it means a lot."

He pressed a kiss to my forehead. "I wanted to." He pulled back. "Now, come on. Despite the fact that this ingredient was hard to get, the potion to give you back control of your magic is easy."

Excitement made my heart race and my soul feel like it wanted to take flight.

Connor unlocked the door to his bar and pulled me inside. Quickly, he flicked on the lights, illuminating the space in a warm glow that highlighted the art on the walls and the sparkling whiskey bottles behind the bar.

His stride was fast as he moved toward the back, and I had to race to keep up. I followed him into a narrow kitchen. He headed toward a door at the rear. Before he walked in, he turned and said, "Could you scrounge up something to eat? I'll get to work on this."

In the little kitchen, I beelined for the fridge, excitement thrumming through me. He might actually be able to get me my power back. *And* we had what we needed to pay off Vlad. Joy burst in my chest as I dug through the fridge, throwing together a couple sandwiches and filling two cups with orange juice. I wanted a beer to celebrate, but we still had work to do.

Loaded down with my loot, I headed through the narrow space to the room where I could hear Connor working. The door was open, revealing a cluttered workroom filled to the brim with tiny bottles, jars, herbs, and tools. Every wall was covered with shelves, and every shelf stuffed full of ingredients. The big table was scarred and covered with various bowls and cauldrons, knives and spoons.

Before entering the workroom, I set the sandwiches on the counter behind me and watched him.

"Almost done." His voice was low with concentration as he bent over a small bowl with a silver knife in hand. "This one just needs to be mixed together. No brewing time required."

I couldn't believe I might be close to finally having control of my magic. It was all I could think about—an all-consuming idea that screamed through my head.

Finally.

A few moments later, he stopped stirring, then reached for a small silver cup. He poured the potion into it, then turned to me, his face tense. "This is it."

I sat up straight. "It's done?"

He nodded and held out the cup full of sparkling blue liquid.

My heart thundered, and I stepped toward him. "Even if this doesn't work, you're my hero for trying."

"I wouldn't mind staying your hero."

I took the cup from him. "I wouldn't mind that, either."

He stepped back. "Go on. The suspense is killing me."

I nodded and put the cup to my lips, my heart pounding. The first sip tasted like apples, and I gulped it down. Adrenaline and hope zipped through my veins as I felt the potion go to work inside me. Magic fizzed through my whole body, and I felt like I'd been filled up with bubbles.

"Well?" Connor asked.

Everything in my body felt more...complete. Like broken pieces were being put back together. A sense of ease I hadn't felt in years swept through me. It was as if everything were the way it should be.

I grinned up at him, hope and elation soaring within, making me feel like I was full of lovely, fizzing bubbles. "I think it's working."

He grinned and hugged me close, pressing a kiss to my mouth.

Magic kept surging through my sinews and muscles, putting me back together again. It was like I'd become so used to being broken I'd forgotten what it was like to feel whole again. Joy filled me up to bursting.

I pulled back from Connor. "I have to test it."

He looked around, then found an old balled-up piece of paper. "Try this."

I took the paper, feeling the crinkly edges against my palm. It grounded me, and when I called upon my magic, the power rushed to life faster and more easily than it had since I'd been cursed.

I set the paper on the ground, then pointed my right index finger at it. When I used to have control of my magic, I could send large or small blasts. This called for a small one. I didn't want to void the floor of his workshop.

The magic sizzled up my arm, and I directed the power toward the paper. It shot from my fingertip as a blast of dark gray smoke, enveloping the paper and sucking it into nothing.

A half second later, the paper was gone.

"It works!" I crowed. "I'll need more practice with bigger things, but it works!"

Connor pulled me into his arms and spun me around. I laughed, excited to try again with something bigger. When I could properly use my talent, I was immensely powerful. Like I'd promised Connor, I could void the weapons of entire armies.

He pressed a kiss to my lips, and I let the pleasure wash over me. When he pulled back, his face was pale. Deathly so. Despite the joy in his eyes, his complexion was ashen.

"Connor? You don't look well." My heart thundered, worry streaking through me.

"I'm fine." His voice was rough, and he had to reach for the wall to steady himself.

"You're not."

"I'm *fine*." He staggered back toward his worktable, nearly going to his knees before he reached the edge.

I hurried after him, panic lighting my heart on fire. "What's wrong?"

"Just a little—" He fumbled with a tiny vial of potion that sat on his counter.

"Let me." I grabbed it and uncorked it, then handed it to him. His hand trembled as he took it. He leaned against the table, his head dipped and shoulders heaving.

I clutched his shoulders. "Connor. Tell me what's wrong!"

"I'm fine." He raised the potion to his lips, staring at it briefly.

"This is what you were talking about. It was deadly to get your wings back." I hated myself for forgetting. My excitement over my own magic had gotten the better of me. Selfish.

Connor swigged the potion, and I waited, heart thundering and prayers racing through my mind.

Please let him be okay.

9

CONNOR

Agony twisted my muscles as the potion went to work inside me. The pain concentrated at my back, where my wings had once lived, and it was so fierce that my vision had gone black.

I'd known when I'd created the potion that it was dangerous. This was worse than I'd expected.

I dragged a hand over my brow and tried to control my breathing.

"I'm the reason you took the potion. Please, Connor. Please be okay."

I could hear the guilt in her voice, but my response was slow to come as the potion worked inside me, repairing the muscles, bones, and organs that were breaking down.

"I just need a moment." My voice was weak, but I could feel the strength slowly returning to my muscles.

The potion wouldn't work forever, but it would hold off the worst of the effects until I could finish the transition process.

"Let me get you to a chair." Sora tugged at my arm, but I resisted.

"I'm fine." My voice was stronger now, thank fates. I blinked, clearing my vision, and stood. Suddenly, my strength returned, and I felt normal. I drew in a deep breath, my muscles relaxing.

"That was a fast-acting potion," Sora said. "You look….fine."

"I feel fine."

"But you aren't fine. Whatever just happened there"—she waved her hand at me—"that was not *fine*."

"Before…when I told you that I gave up my wings, I gave up the magic inside them as well. I never told my sister that my wings were unusual. We were teenagers then, and the whole…" I waved my hand. "Puberty thing. New magic was appearing inside me, but we were so busy dealing with the Court trying to evict her that I didn't want to mention it."

"You're the best brother."

I didn't do so hot with compliments, so I ignored her words. "Anyway, I created and drank a potion that got rid of my wings and the magic within them."

"And now you've taken the potion to bring them back," Sora said. "But you said that it was deadly."

I turned to her, catching sight of the worry in her eyes. Her brow was creased, and her mouth turned down, but she was still cute as hell. "The potion I took to get my wings back...it was just the start of the process."

"What do you mean?" she asked.

"It's a two-part potion. The first one gave me my wings back, but not the magic within them. Without that magic, I am incomplete, and the wings are destroying my body."

Sora turned white. "Destroying?"

"Breaking it down to feed themselves. I have a potion that will hold it off, but not forever. The only thing that will fix me for good is the second potion, which will give my wings their magic back. When they are complete, they'll stop destroying me."

"So you need to finish the potion?" Sora looked around as if she'd find the components here and wanted to whip it up herself. Despite the impossibility of it, something thudded in my chest at the idea that she would try to fix me.

"Yes. But I don't have the ingredients. Not because I didn't want to be prepared, but because I couldn't. The spell requires my newly transformed blood, plus an ingredient that has an extremely limited shelf life."

"So we have to go get this ingredient and combine it with your new blood, then you're fixed?" Sora asked.

"Basically." It wasn't as easy as that, but if I told her that, she'd insist on coming, and that would be too dangerous.

An image of the burning village from my dreams flickered in my mind, but I shoved it away. I had no idea why it haunted me, and I didn't have time to think of it now.

"So let's go get the ingredient. It's rare, but surely the Sorcerer's Guild must have it. You saw all that stuff!" Her brow furrowed. "But you went for my stuff first. To give me my power back."

"Of course. But the Sorcerer's Guild doesn't have what I need. No shop or Guild does." I dragged a hand over my face. How much to tell her? How many of my secrets to reveal? Even Claire didn't know all of them. "I'm going to go deal with this, and I'll find you when I'm done, all right?"

"Oh, *hell* no. You are insane if you think I'm leaving you like this to fix yourself."

"I'll be fine. If I take a restorative draught every twelve hours or so, I'll stay strong enough to finish this." I didn't mention that the draught would stop working at some point. Then I'd be dead in…oh, say two days. Maybe less.

Either way, it'd be painful as hell.

"You fixed me." Her voice was hard as steel. "Now I'm going to help fix you."

"You don't have to."

"I don't freaking care." She glared at me, sizing me up. "You said you haven't told your sister about this."

"Not quite." There was a lot I hadn't told my sister. Mostly to protect her.

Sora nodded, appearing satisfied. "Exactly. So if you don't let me help you, you'd better believe I'm going to rat you out to your sister in about two seconds flat."

I sighed, tilting my head back. Claire deserved to know. I couldn't argue that point. But I didn't need her worrying about me. Between her and Sora, their concern would crush me.

I'd rather deal with one worried woman. And I couldn't lie—Sora was powerful, and her magic was useful. If I only had a couple days left, I wanted to spend them with her.

"Fine," I said. "Thank you."

Her brows rose. "You're letting me help?"

"I'm not an idiot. You're strong and smart. And I could use the assistance."

"And you don't want me to tell your sister."

"I'll tell my sister one day. When this is over and I'm safe. But mostly, I just want to be with you."

Concern flashed in her eyes. "Shit. Are you worried you're going to die?"

"No." A little. "It'll be fine. Just difficult."

"I can't believe you did this for me."

The image of her falling replayed in my mind. I gripped her arms and pulled her toward me, meeting her gaze. "Of course I did. I couldn't watch you die."

She swallowed hard, her throat moving. Something passed between us, a tension that tightened the air and made me want to lean down and kiss her. But there was no time, and if I started, I wouldn't stop.

"Shit." A horrible thought occurred. "The potion for the Devil of Darkvale. We need to make that."

"When we're done with this." Sora's voice was firm.

"He can wait?" It would take nearly a day to brew. We didn't have a day.

"He's going to have to. We need to get started on fixing you. There's no time to waste."

She was right. There just wasn't time—not if I wanted to survive.

I nodded, almost reluctantly, then pointed to the plants that we'd grown in the Sorcerer's Guild. They were laid out on the table. "The main ingredient is here. If I don't...make it, you can get someone to create the potion. There are some Blood Sorceresses in Darklane who should be able to help. My sister can find them for you."

She ignored my words and tugged on me. "We should go. Where to?"

"London."

"Back there? Really?"

"Yes. Not your part, though." There were many magical parts to London. Guild City was just one of them. Fletcher's Wine Bar was another, though we weren't going for the wine.

"Lead the way." Sora gestured to the spot on the shelves where I kept the transport charms.

I pulled my leather jacket off the post on the wall and tugged it on, then grabbed a bag and stuffed it with potions of all varieties. I had no idea what I'd need, so I filled it to the brim. Once it was ready, I stashed it in the ether and shoved some of the restorative draughts into my pocket, bringing all that I had.

Finally, I grabbed one of the transport charms and

turned to Sora. "I need to go lock the door to the bar. We can leave from there."

She nodded and turned to leave my workshop. Two sandwiches sat on a plate on the counter, and she grabbed them both. "Here." She shoved one toward me. "I forgot I made them."

My stomach growled at the sight, and I took it. "Thank you."

She nodded. We ate as I led the way through the narrow kitchen, out to the main bar. Just as I reached the front door, Claire opened it and stepped inside.

"What's going on?" My sister's voice echoed with worry. "The shop looks closed, and it's breakfast time."

Shit. The last bite of sandwich went down a bit hard.

Our friend Cass entered behind Claire, her red hair gleaming in the light.

This was the last thing I needed. Two concerned women. Three, if I counted Cass, which I should. She was like family, and if she got a whiff that Claire was concerned, she would be, too.

Claire wore her black leather pants and top, her dark hair pulled back from her face. It was her usual fight-wear. Cass was dressed in the jeans and leather jacket she considered a uniform. Both were splattered with something that looked like blood. There was no telling what they'd been up to. Either a demon hunt as part of Claire's occasional gig as a mercenary or Cass's work as a magic hunter.

"Connor? Are you all right?" Claire asked. "This is unusual."

"Bridgette's coming in," I said, referring to the part-time staffer who worked Potions & Pastilles when we couldn't.

"Yeah. But something is still wrong." Claire's gaze flicked to my new companion.

"This is Sora." I gestured to her, knowing that it would distract Claire. I rarely brought women to P&P, which was essentially my home, and my sister was a bloodhound determined to find me someone to settle down with. Since Sora was my fated mate, Claire would be *very* interested to meet her.

"Hi." Claire smiled widely and stuck out her hand. "I'm Claire."

Cass stuck out her hand as well. "I'm Cass."

Sora shook both hands, shooting a look between me and my sister. I could tell that Claire was going to want to settle down for a long chat, but we needed to get a move on.

"We have something we need to do," I said.

Claire's gaze moved to mine, and her eyes narrowed. "Something is wrong. You can't fool me."

No, I couldn't. Not even with bait like Sora. But I could keep her busy.

"It's important, and I don't have time to explain," I said. "Can you visit Orion and tell him we're going to need two mounts?"

"Why do you need to go to the Fire Fae Court?" She

frowned. "You hate it there."

I couldn't explain that I needed water from the Sacred Sea, a small, magical body of water hidden deep in Dartmoor. "I just do. I'll explain it later. Please."

She grumbled. "I don't like not knowing, but I'll ask Orion. Where are you going?"

That was another secret. I'd kept too many, and suddenly, I regretted it. It'd been easy for years, and since it had allowed us to focus on the challenges she faced, it had seemed like a good idea. But those secrets were about to become a whole lot harder to keep.

I hesitated briefly. "London."

"Where I'm from," Sora said, implying it was on a job for her.

I could have kissed her.

"Fine." Sora looked between us. "Be careful."

"Thank you." I gave her a quick hug, then looked at Sora. "Ready to get out of here?"

She nodded, then turned to Claire and Cass. "Nice to meet you."

"Nice to meet you, too. You seem cool. We should have a drink sometime." Claire grinned widely. It was obvious from the keen brightness to her eyes that she was ravenous for details. Sora wouldn't notice, but I'd known Claire forever. She wanted info.

"We're going now, sis."

"Right. Of course. Go on." She kept grinning, displaying an extreme lack of chill.

I looked away. It was the only logical option.

Sora reached for my hand, and I took hers, my fingers closing over her daintier ones. She was so much smaller than me that I couldn't help but worry about her, even though I knew she was strong as hell.

"Bye, sis. Bye, Cass." I chucked the transport charm on the ground.

The silver smoke poofed upward, glittering in the air. I envisioned the entrance to Fletcher's Wine Bar, located near the Thames, and stepped into the smoke, letting the ether suck me in and whip me around. It pulled us through space, making my head spin slightly. Within seconds, my feet were on the cobblestone walkway outside of the bar. Sora appeared next to me.

Fletcher's was one of the oldest bars in London, built into the storage tunnels beneath one of the mansions situated along the Thames. It'd been in the same family for over a century, and even though humans sometimes patronized the establishment, it was a common supernatural hangout. No obvious wings, horns, or fangs allowed, of course. Only supernaturals who could pass for humans.

"The Thames is just over there." I gestured toward the embankment behind us. We couldn't see the river, as it was hidden behind the brick wall and piled-up dirt that had been added about a century and a half ago, but it was there.

We stood in an outdoor alley, bordered by the embankment on one side and the bar on the other. A hostess stood at a podium near the door, her dark hair pulled neatly back into a ponytail. Though there was no sign that she was a Magica, I knew she was. They were the only ones who worked here.

"Are we going in?" Sora asked.

"Yes." I strode toward the hostess, Sora at my side. When we reached her, I leaned close and said, "I'll need the train as soon as possible."

Her eyes flickered with knowledge and she nodded. "Of course, sir. I'll find you a table while you wait."

I could feel Sora's confusion as the hostess led us into the bar. The place was a warren of tunnels and tables, and the bartenders manning the bar had the bored expressions of guys who were trying too hard. We followed the hostess through the dark space, the low, arched ceiling brushing the top of my hair. Tiny tables were cluttered around, each with a single, dripping red wax candle.

"It's a shame this place has no atmosphere," Sora murmured beside me.

I laughed low in my throat. Fletcher's was one of the most charming places in London.

The hostess found us the best table in the place, situated in the very back. It was darkly shadowed and private, and would be romantic if not for the real reason we were here.

She sat us. "I'll bring you the usual, sir. The train will be here shortly."

She spoke quietly enough that none of the other patrons could hear, but Sora tilted her head as she listened, her brow furrowed.

The hostess disappeared, and Sora looked at me. "Train?"

I leaned close enough to speak right onto her ear, and she shivered. Heat raced down my spine, and I wished that we weren't on a race for my life. I'd rather drink two bottles of wine with her here, sharing kisses and then a walk along the Thames. Followed by a night at the Savoy nearby.

I pitched my voice low as I spoke. "This is a bar, yes. But it's also the entrance to a train station that's located under the river."

"You're kidding me."

"I'm not." I leaned back and met her gaze, trying to let her see the seriousness of my expression.

The hostess arrived with a bottle of wine and filled two glasses. I hadn't even bothered to ask what Sora wanted. Shit.

"I'm sorry I didn't ask what you wanted. It's a bit autopilot here," I said when the hostess left, and I gestured to the bottle. "I don't actually like this much myself. She just always brings it."

The corner of her mouth tugged up. "We're not here for the wine, anyway."

"That's the truth."

"Why don't you tell me more, then? Where the hell are we going?"

My gaze flicked around the room. I'd already said too much. Though it had been quiet, I couldn't risk more. Not until we were on the train. The penalty for revealing the existence of the Arcane Order of Alchemists was steep—death.

I picked up my wine. "I promise I'll tell you as soon as we get to the train."

She gave me a long stare. "Fine. I trust you." She looked around. "Anyway, I like an adventure."

I took a sip of my wine, suddenly feeling exhausted. Fates, I hoped we could rest a while on the train.

We only had to wait about ten minutes, fortunately. I didn't drink much of my wine. It'd take a hell of a lot more to mess me up, but I needed my wits about me. And I didn't know how it would react now that I had the potion racing through my blood.

The hostess appeared like a ghost. "The train is ready."

I nodded and thanked her, then stood. I left a tip on the table, but the wine was covered by the Order. Sora joined me, and we followed the hostess toward the only empty tunnel in the whole bar. A door said that it was storage, but there was nothing inside except another door and a guard at the far end.

The hostess led us toward the guard, departing as we reached him.

The man was huge—at least seven feet tall and as broad as a house. His magic sparked around him, tiny golden flecks that screamed *threat*.

He nodded his head at me. "Alchemist."

Sora shot me a look, and I could read her thoughts. *See! I knew you were an Alchemist.*

"Terrence." I nodded. I rarely visited the Arcane Order, but I'd seen him before.

He reached forward with his enormous hands, and I raised my chin, letting him press his fingertips to my temples. I could feel the tendrils of his magic seeping inside my mind, searching for any kind of threat to the Arcane Order.

He would find none. I'd joined willingly and respected their rules.

When he was finished, he lowered his hands and nodded.

I looked down at Sora. "He's going to use his magic to check your intentions."

"I don't even know where I'm going."

"For the best," Terrence rumbled.

"You can still do your thing?" Sora asked.

"Always." He reached for her, and she stood still as he touched her temples. I squeezed her hand, but she didn't seem worried.

She trusts me.

It was a heavy burden. Even though I knew I'd never betray her, I couldn't protect her from everything, no matter how much I wanted to. The idea made me want to climb out of my skin. Hell, I thought I wanted to follow her around for the rest of her life making sure she didn't get hit by a bus, but I knew she wouldn't tolerate that.

Terrence lowered his hands. "You're fine. The train is waiting."

"Thank you," I said, nodding again.

He opened the door, and I stepped through, leading Sora into another tunnel. It was empty and dark, with only weak lamplight flickering over the damp bricks. The tunnel sloped downward, heading deep underground.

As soon as the door shut behind us, Sora spoke. "Right. You're going to have to cough up the info now, buddy."

I smiled as I led her down the tunnel. "Fair enough. I'm a member of the Arcane Order of Alchemists."

"Never heard of it."

"That's the point."

"Okay, that makes sense. Why are we going?"

"I'll need a specific—and rare—set of tools to make the potion that will give me back my magic. They're ancient and valuable, and thus, they are held by the Arcane Order. I need to get permission to take them. Then, we'll go find the final ingredient for the potion that will cure me."

"That will be on Dartmoor?"

"Yes. How'd you know?" Then I remembered. "Ah, you heard me tell my sister to go there."

"Yep. So, what does the Arcane Order of Alchemists do?"

"It's a group of the most powerful potion masters in the world. Highly secretive. The things that we have the ability to create could change the world—for better or worse. Much of it for worse."

"Then why do you create it?"

"We don't. Not normally. But if we were discovered for our skills, we could be forced to do great damage. And so we remain secret."

She waved her hand around the tunnel. "Hence this whole thing."

"Exactly. The location of the headquarters of the Arcane Order changes regularly. Only those who live there know where it is located. The rest of us come here and take the train. With any luck, the ride will be long enough that we can get a few hours of sleep."

"Why don't you live there?"

"I don't want to." We were nearly to the station, and I could hear the rumble of the old steam train. "They tried to force me to, but I wouldn't leave my sister. Their only alternative was to give me my way or kill me."

"And you're too powerful and valuable to kill."

"I like to think so. Also, I have powerful friends." I exited the tunnel into the enormous cavern that contained the train. The room was dark and damp, and the train sat right in the middle. It was a beautiful black and red piece of the past, and though it was partially run by steam, it was also powered by magic.

Sora stopped dead in her tracks and gasped. "I can't believe this was down here and I didn't know."

"Almost no one does."

"Not even your sister?" she asked.

"I never told her."

"Why not?"

"She would have wanted me to pursue it more, thinking it was my passion. She'd have felt guilty that I'd stayed with her."

"To protect her."

I nodded. "We needed to focus on what she was facing. I didn't want to be anywhere else, anyway. But she already had guilt over me leaving our Court for her. She didn't need this."

"You should tell her."

I almost said *no*. But Sora was right. Claire had fulfilled her destiny and saved our people. She'd found her fated mate. There was no reason for me to stay silent to protect her anymore, and the lies wouldn't sit well with her.

"I'll tell her when we're done."

"Promise?"

"Promise."

I reached the entrance to the train, and the porter, Ryan, bowed to me. He was a skinny guy, with a flat-top hat and old-style uniform. Despite his unassuming appearance, I could feel the magic radiating from him.

"Alchemist." His voice echoed with respect.

"Ryan."

"The journey will be six hours. There is a sleeper car made up for you."

I could have wept, I was so grateful. I couldn't remember the last time I'd slept, and the potion coursing through me was enough to make me feel weak, despite the gift of my wings.

"Thank you."

"Will you need two cars?" he asked.

I almost said yes, but Sora spoke. "How big is the bed?"

"Big enough for two."

She looked at me. "Just sleeping."

"Fine by me." It'd take me longer to fall asleep if she were pressed up against me, but hell would freeze before I said no to that offer.

Ryan led us to an opulently decorated sleeper cabin. It was done up in the same red and black as the exterior of the train, the bed covered with a velvet duvet. I barely got my shoes off before I fell into the bed. Sora lay down, and I tugged her against me, wanting to feel her warmth.

As the train chugged out of the station, she sighed and curled up against my side. "This is moving fast."

"Sixty miles an hour."

"You know what I mean."

I nodded. I did, and I liked it that way.

10

Sora

I woke to the feel of Connor's warm chest beneath my cheek and the rumble of the train as it pulled to a stop.

I yawned, not wanting to wake Connor but knowing I had to. He'd seemed fine since he'd taken the potion, but his pale face and shaky demeanor had scared the crap out of me. He was so strong and powerful—the idea that anything could take him down was terrifying.

My mind drifted back to meeting his sister. I'd liked her right away. Same for the other girl, Cass. I'd barely spoken to them, but I'd felt...something. Like we could be friends.

"We're here." His voice was rough with sleep.

"You're awake?"

"Yeah. Felt us stop." He pulled me close and pressed a

kiss to my forehead, and I couldn't help the surge of warmth that filled my chest.

This was nice.

Really nice.

I sat up, and he followed.

"Is it dangerous in there?" I asked.

"Not particularly. You're with me, which means you're fine while we're inside. However..." He pulled his potion bag from the ether and dug through it, then retrieved a tiny bottle made of green glass and handed it to me. "Take that. It will make it so that no one remembers your face once you've left."

"Wow." I inspected the vial appreciatively.

"Try not to speak much if you can help it," he said. "Not that you wouldn't have something valuable to say, but it will give them less to remember."

"So, I'm safe while I'm in there with you. But once I've left..."

"No guarantees. Especially if you're not with me. But that potion will hide you. You'll be safe after you leave."

I nodded. "Secret societies are intense."

"That's the truth. I trust most of the alchemists, but there are a few who I don't. And you just never can tell."

"What kind of Magica are they?" I drank the potion, shivering at the bitter taste.

"Many are Fae. We have a gift for potions. But there are some witches and sorcerers as well. A shifter or two."

He took my empty potion vial and put it in his bag,

then stashed the whole thing in the ether. He tugged on his shoes, and I did the same.

"I trust that you can handle yourself in there," Connor said. "I don't think anything will go wrong, but you have my support to void the whole place if you feel threatened."

I squeezed his hand. "Aw. You say the sweetest things."

"What can I say? I like you."

"More than your secret society."

"Society of moody old alchemists, yes. The competition isn't fierce. But I'd like you even if they were Amy MacDonald."

"Who, the singer? You like?"

"Love." He winked. "Now, come on. Let's go face the beast and figure out the next step of this adventure."

"I like going on an adventure with you. But it'd be better if you weren't fighting for your life."

"I'll be fine. There's no real risk."

I knew he was lying. Could hear it in his voice. He *would* be fine, but only if we got the stuff he needed to fix himself. If we didn't....

I couldn't even think of it.

Hell, I didn't need to. I would fix this for him if the potion made him too weak.

Connor led me out into another train station. Cold wind whipped across my face, and the night was dark. We were outside, and there was nearly no light. The station itself was tiny, just a platform built onto the top of a mountain. In the distance, I spotted an enormous stone tower. The full moon rose behind it, illuminating it in silver light.

"It looks like a freaking haunted fairytale," I muttered.

"They have a flare for the dramatic." Lightning struck behind the tower, illuminating it in bright white light. "Just on time."

There was something strange in Connor's voice, but before I could ask, he'd taken my hand and tugged me toward the stairs that led down from the platform.

The slender young man who'd first greeted us on the train held open the wrought iron gate to let us leave.

"Thanks, Ryan," Connor said.

I smiled at him as we walked down the stairs to the simple stone pathway that led to the tower. It was only about a hundred yards away, surrounded on all sides by spiky gray bits of mountain. The cold wind tugged my hair back from my face and sneaked under my jacket, making me shiver hard.

Connor tugged off his jacket and handed it to me.

"I can't take that." I pushed it back to him.

He draped it over my shoulders, then pulled me against the warmth of his side. We matched steps easily and strode up the path to the castle.

"If these folks ever run out of money, they can totally rent this place out to Hollywood. It'd be great for a Frankenstein remake."

He chuckled. "I'll let them know."

"I suppose that's too low-class for the Ancient Order of Alchemists, though." I grinned. "And they can make gold."

"Yes."

"Can you make gold?"

"Yes."

"Do you?"

"No. Not often. And there are a lot of rules around it. We're each only allowed to make so much of it—both by law and the rules of finite magic—but I make some and donate it when I can."

Warmth surged through me. "That's lovely."

"Not sure I'd go that far. But I'd be a real asshole if I ignored a gift that could help people."

"You're a good dude, Connor."

He gave me a skeptical look, but we were nearly to the entrance, so he said nothing.

The tower loomed overhead, rising at least a hundred feet in the air. It was stark and creepy, even without the lighting slicing through the air behind it. The Sorcerer's Tower in Guild City suddenly looked a lot less scary.

There were no guards at the huge door, but it glowed with faint green magic that made me nervous. Connor strode up the wide stairs, and as we reached the top, three guards drifted through the wood of the door. They glowed with green light, and their eyes were deep as emeralds. Their uniforms were stark black chain mail, and they each carried a sword and shield.

But their magic...

Holy fates, their magic made me feel like I was going to be knocked over. They were insanely powerful, and I wasn't used to supernaturals letting it all hang out like that.

The three of them looked from Connor to me.

"Let her in," Connor said, his voice quietly commanding.

The three guards nodded in unison, then drifted back through the door like ghosts. A moment later, the door's green glow faded, leaving only stark black wood. It swung open silently, revealing a massive entry hall that gleamed with golden light.

Connor took my hand, and I followed him in, awed by the riches around me. The walls themselves were draped with thick black fabric, but everything else was made of gold—furniture, light fixtures, even the artwork.

Connor leaned down to speak close to my ear, and I shivered as heat streaked through me. "You see why I don't want to live here?"

"Yeah. This is…a lot."

"Too much." He straightened and looked around, clearly waiting for someone.

I took of his jacket and returned it to him. He shrugged it back on.

A figure appeared through a doorway on the other side, her form slender and tall. She was draped in gorgeous golden fabric, and even though I didn't like the decor in this place, I had to admit that she looked fab.

"That's Lucretia," Connor murmured. "One of the oldest members of the Ancient Order."

She glided toward us so gracefully that it looked like she was floating. As she neared, I got a better look at her face. She had warm brown skin and gorgeous golden eyes that matched her dress. Her head had been shaved to a smooth shine, and she was so beautiful that I swore she couldn't possibly be from Earth. Her magic rolled out from her on waves of light, making her glow like a star. She was insanely powerful, and I vowed not to get on her bad side. I was no weakling, but she could crush me like a bug.

"Connor." Her voice was warm, and her eyes glinted with more heat as they scanned up and down his body.

I wanted to growl at her but bit it back. *Down, girl.* I was being ridiculous. But this lady clearly wanted a bite of Connor, and I was not having it.

"Lucretia." His voice was formal and distant, so unlike the voice he used to speak with me. It made me feel better.

"You brought a guest." Her eyes flickered over me and our joined hands, then widened. "You've given her a face concealment potion."

"I did."

"Hmm." She looked disappointed. "You must care for her. Those are valuable."

I looked toward Connor, and he nodded. "I do. I'm here to meet with the Council."

"Why?" Her gaze traveled over him again, and she gasped. "You didn't."

"I did."

"You knew that potion was dangerous."

"I did."

"I did? That's all you can say?" She sounded angry now. "You risked your life. For what?"

He said nothing, and she nodded, her eyes going to me. "Of course. You've found her, then."

Found her? I desperately wanted to ask, but I remembered what he'd said about staying quiet. This woman was so powerful, and she was too interested in Connor. I didn't need her coming after me.

"Can we call a meeting?" Connor asked. "You understand that time is of the essence."

"Of course." She snapped to attention, spinning on her heel and stalking across the room. "I'll wake everyone and have them gathered in the meeting hall in ten minutes."

Her swift change of pace made me nervous. Clearly, this was a huge deal. She was genuinely scared for Connor.

"Come." Connor tugged on my hand, and I followed him.

I hurried to keep up with his long strides, and I had a feeling that he was trying to outrun my questions as much as anything.

"Found her?" I asked.

"Lucretia is dramatic."

There was something in his voice that made me wonder about the truth of that—she was dramatic, sure, but she hadn't seemed dramatic at that moment. But then we entered a hallway where other figures were walking, and now wasn't the time to discuss it.

Connor led me through a maze of hallways until we reached a huge room near the back of the castle. A massive square table sat in the middle, surrounded on all sides by chairs—forty in all.

The Ancient Order must be large.

There were several figures already sitting at the table,

most of them draped in gold cloth like Lucretia had been. Each cloth was a slightly different shade, from burnished gold to rose, but the wealth of the place was unmistakable. It was well past midnight, but they all looked perfect.

I found I preferred Connor in his T-shirt and jeans.

Each of the figures nodded at Connor, and we took a seat at the side of the table that was empty. We were as far away from the others as we could possibly be.

"To avoid small talk," Connor murmured against my ear, so low that only I could hear.

I couldn't imagine what small talk these weirdos would be capable of, and I found myself grateful for the thought.

As we waited for the rest to arrive, I studied everyone in the room, trying to get a hint at what they were. As he'd said, many of them were Fae. Their pointed ears and eerie beauty made that clear. But there were others as well—mages and shifters and witches. They weren't shy about letting their magical signature radiate from them, and the whole room was filled with the scents and sounds of magic.

The table filled quickly, and my heart began to pound.

Everyone looked worried.

Like, really worried.

I gripped Connor's hand under the table. He squeezed back, as if knowing I needed something to anchor me.

It wasn't all these scary bastards that made me nervous. I could probably cause enough havoc with my void magic to make a run for it if I needed to.

No, it was the concern on their faces. I shot Connor a glance, weirded out to see him completely expressionless.

This was another Connor. Not the one I knew.

Finally, the table was full. Across from us, a ghostly woman sat still as a statue, her form partially transparent. Her features were soft and faded, like an old painting, and it was impossible to tell if she was even alive. She might actually be a ghost, though she glowed with a golden light that was unlike any ghost I'd ever seen.

She leaned forward and looked straight at Connor. "You need the tools of the Rising One."

"I do."

"How long do you have?"

"I took the potion about seven hours ago."

She cursed. "You knew that was a dangerous potion."

"It's my specialty, isn't it?"

"There is no turning back from this, you know." Her voice cracked like a whip. "You may not live long enough to use the tools to save yourself, and then where will we be?"

"I'll live long enough."

"We'll see." She waved a hand over the table in front of her, and a small cauldron appeared. It, too, was semi-transparent, and the smoke that wafted up from it gleamed with pale light.

She leaned over it and peered into the depths, her brow wrinkling. She conjured small bottles in her hands, pouring them into the cauldron and stirring it with a silver knife. Then she spat in it. I cringed. *Gross.*

"We will test your strength, Alchemist, and see if you

are worthy to walk into the flames." She waved a hand, and the cauldron drifted across the table toward him. It glided to a stop, and a small ladle appeared next to it.

Connor dipped it in and drank. His eyes unfocused, and his brow creased.

Pain spiked my insides, and I doubled over. Gasping, I struggled to right myself. Next to me, Connor sat dead still, but his fists were clenched by his sides.

He was in pain, too. Terrible pain. Somehow, I knew it. And I was feeling it, too.

What the hell was happening?

Connor raised his hands and reached for the silver knife that sat by the cauldron. It hadn't been there when I'd looked last.

He sliced into his wrist, letting the red blood flow into the cauldron that he'd just drunk from. He lowered his hands, and the cauldron began to smoke. It drifted back toward the middle of the table, and the pale gray smoke turned a deep navy blue.

There were murmurs from the crowd as they watched it, and the ghostly woman nodded, her brows raised. "It seems you are indeed strong enough to possibly survive."

"We've never seen midnight blue before," murmured a woman near me, sounding awed.

Connor must be extremely powerful, if their reaction was anything to go by.

"You have earned the right to use the tools of the Rising One." She leaned forward, her voice deep and dark. "But if you live through this and succeed, be prepared to face what you really are, Storm Bringer. There is no turning back from this much power."

What you really are? Storm Bringer?

Connor had more secrets. Did this have to do with the magic that was in his wings? I'd assumed it was just more power of the same kind he already had. But maybe not. Maybe it was something new.

Hell, how many secrets did this guy have?

11

Connor

After the meeting, most of the alchemists fled quickly, as if they didn't want to be near a dead man walking.

Fair enough. The potion I'd made to fix my wings was just as likely to kill me as anything. Many of the alchemists were immortal, and the mere idea of mortality made them itchy.

I turned to Sora. "We need to go to the armory at the base of the castle, then we can leave."

She nodded and stood.

I joined her. "This way."

I approached a tall man who stood by the door. Farrow was also Fae, and he was the keeper of the keys to the armory. As we stopped before him, he stared at me with a heavy expression in his green eyes. His pale blond hair was pulled back in a long tail, and his simple warrior's clothing was green instead of the usual gold.

Farrow wasn't a bad guy, even though I found him to be a bit strange. Anyone who sought immortality was weird, as far as I was concerned, as I'd never met a single one of them that was happy. It seemed to do something to them, sucking the joy from their lives.

"Farrow." I nodded in greeting, stepping partially in front of Sora. I knew she could take care of herself, but still, it made me nervous to have her near the rest of the Ancient Order.

"Connor." His lips twisted slightly on the word. He didn't like calling me by my chosen name, but I'd insisted once. With my fist.

It was a lesson he hadn't forgotten.

"Thank you for taking us to the armory."

His hand brushed over the cluster of gold keys that hung on his belt, and he nodded. "This way."

We followed him through the dark hallways, the cold stone watching us as we walked.

Sora leaned close and whispered, "Do they have to switch castles every time they move as well?"

"No. The castle itself moves. This building is ancient." I recalled the mountains outside the window. "I believe we are in Wales, close to the original place where the Arcane Order was founded."

"Not too far from Dartmoor, then."

"Thank fates."

Farrow turned a corner and approached a wide staircase that led downward. His footsteps were silent as he descended, the golden torchlight gleaming off his fair hair. We followed, reaching an enormous wooden door.

The protective magic that surrounded the door felt like knives against the skin—by far, the most powerful protective charm I'd ever felt. Worse even than the entry to the castle itself.

Sora cringed backward. "Holy crap, that's powerful. What have you got in there, the secret to eternal life?"

Farrow looked back at her, brow raised. "Close enough. Forget you've ever been here."

The coldness in his voice made me step forward.

He glared at me and turned back to the door, fiddling with his keyring.

I was glad I'd given Sora the potion to conceal her face. Farrow and I would never crack open a beer together, but that wasn't why he didn't like her being here. I hadn't technically broken the rules, but many of the members of the Arcane Order were ridiculously secretive. Living cooped up here for so many years, some of them immortal, made them crazy.

Farrow's key clicked in the lock, and the protective spell faded from the door. He pushed it open, and we followed him into a long, massive room. The walls were covered in all variety of weapons, though the Arcane Order's members rarely used them. All were enchanted somehow, which was where their real value lay. More often than not, they sold or traded them.

Sora looked around, then whistled low under her breath. "Nice collection."

"It's not even the good part," I said.

Farrow led us to the end of the room, where the wall was concealed by a dark, hazy mist. It was impossible to see beyond it, and Sora faltered.

"It's all right." I gripped her hand.

She squeezed tight.

Farrow walked through the mist, and I followed. Sora kept up, barely hesitating even though we couldn't see a foot in front of our faces.

A few steps later, we entered an enormous, domed room. In the middle, a fire roared. It was as least fifteen feet tall and just as wide, with no wood or any other kind of fuel at the bottom. The flames flickered orange and gold, burning impossibly bright. The heat seared my face, and I stepped in front of Sora to block her.

She peered out from behind my shoulder. "What the hell?"

"This is the Flame of the Rising One," Farrow said to her.

I'd never actually stepped into the flame—that was exceedingly rare—but I knew what it was.

"It's where the ancient tools are stored," he continued. "Connor will enter to retrieve them."

Sora yanked on my hand. "You're going to walk in there?"

I nodded. The heat was insanely intense, and would remain so even after I walked into the flame. The test I'd just completed at the meeting table had proven that I'd survive, but I certainly wouldn't enjoy it.

Farrow took up his position near the wall, and I nodded toward him. "You can go join him," I told Sora. "It won't take long."

"I don't like this." Worry flickered in her eyes.

"I'm used to this. Don't worry." It was only partially a lie. I wasn't old hat at walking into fire, but it would be fine.

She scowled at me, and tension hung in the air for the briefest second. Then she leaned forward and pressed a hard kiss to my lips.

Surprise—and desire—flashed inside me, and I yanked her close, my hand behind her back. I kissed her briefly, and she kissed me back before pulling away, still glaring. "Be careful."

I nodded, head spinning slightly. This thing between us was moving a hell of a lot faster than I'd expected.

She turned and walked toward Farrow, staying far from the flame as she approached him and stood pressed against the wall. I gave her one last look, then strode to the other side of the room where a pedestal waited.

A massive stone bowl sat on top of it, filled to the brim with a glittering blue liquid. A ladle hung on a silver hook, and I removed it, then dipped the spoon in to the liquid. It gleamed blue and bright as I raised it to my lips and drank.

Ice flowed through my veins, and I shivered hard as I returned the ladle. I wouldn't have long, and it wouldn't keep me from feeling all of the fire's burn, but it should keep me alive and uninjured.

In theory.

Chilled to the bone, I turned and strode to the fire, not looking at Sora. I didn't want to see her wide eyes and pale face. Given the choice, I'd rather make her happy than scared.

But first, I had to live. And that required getting the tools of the Rising One.

The fire blazed in front of me, bright and fierce. The heat was impossible, making my eyes water and every inch of me burn. I sucked in a deep breath and strode into it, nearly going to my knees from the agony. The flames licked at my skin, and the pain was enough to make my mind go blank. For the briefest second, I had no idea why I was there. Every inch of me felt like it was melting, and in the distance, I heard Sora scream.

It jerked me back to the present, and I kept going, staggering to the middle of the fire. As I walked, images flashed in my mind.

The unknown village. It was a simple place, full of Fae living in a valley. I didn't know them beyond the visions I'd had for years.

Drought had leeched the life from their land, turning the earth barren and beige. Fire raged in the distance, creeping toward their town.

Somehow, it was real.

Except I had no idea who they were or when it happened. The fear for them—the helplessness—stole my breath.

I shook the thoughts away, focusing on the task at hand. I wouldn't be driven away by weakness and fear.

Storm Bringer.

The flame seemed to whisper to me.

That was twice now that I'd heard the title. Before this, I hadn't heard it in years, not since a spirit had whispered it to me when I'd been a boy changing into a man.

When I reached the middle of the fire, I knelt. There, sitting on the ground in the middle of the flame, were the tools of the Rising One: a small cauldron, knife, and set of measuring spoons.

So simple, yet so powerful.

I could barely see them through the flickering flames.

No one knew how old they were. Centuries, at least. They'd been imbued with the power of many ancient alchemists, these flames keeping that magic alive. They were the most powerful potion-making tools in the world, and they were necessary for what was to come.

I picked them up, my strength flagging, and staggered onward. I just needed to get out of the fire...

Every step seemed to take the last of my strength. I wasn't melting or burning alive, but it was sapping my power.

Finally, I reached the edge. When I exited, the air was immediately cooler. I sucked in a deep breath and focused my dry eyes.

Sora stood in front of me, face pale and eyes dark. "Are you okay?" Her gaze searched me, and she swallowed hard.

"Fine." My voice was dry. The tools of the Rising One

were still clutched in my hands, and I looked down. I needed to put them away.

I shook my head, trying to get my thoughts back in line as I pulled an empty bag from the ether and added the tools. They clinked against the tiny vials of ingredients that were already measured out, ready for me to create the potion that would heal me. Quickly, I closed the bag, then stored it carefully away again.

"Are you sure you're okay?" Sora sounded skeptical. She ran her hands down my arms, seeming like she was checking to see if I was still in one piece.

I looked down at myself, still feeling the burn of the flames. I looked fine. Clothes and skin unburned. I still felt a bit woozy, but that was all right. "I'm fine. Let's get out of here."

"Those are the best words I've heard all day." Her gaze flicked to the flame behind me. "You alchemists are crazy."

I grinned, then grabbed her hand, and we joined Farrow by the door.

He was silent as he led us out of the room and up the stairs. I was ready to get the hell out of the armory.

We reached the top of the stairs that had led down to the Flame of the Rising One. Farrow stopped. "This is where I leave you. Good luck with your journey."

"Thank you." I nodded to him, then turned.

Sora and I walked quickly through the wide corridors, and I felt like my heels were on fire. We reached the exterior doors and the guards opened them, and I took the main stairs two at a time. Sora kept up easily, and when we were on the main path, she leaned up and spoke against my ear. "You don't like that place."

"Not much, no. But being a member provides me with access to tools that I wouldn't have otherwise."

"No kidding."

The train waited at the station, steam billowing from the stack. Ryan opened the gate to the platform, then hurried ahead and opened the door to one of the train cars.

We climbed into the dining car, and I found a seat. Sora sat across from me, slumping in her chair.

"Hungry?" I asked.

She nodded. "Ravenous."

Ryan hovered near the entrance to the dining car, his gaze alert on mine. I nodded to him, and he hurried off to the kitchen.

Sora raised her brows. "Fancy."

"It's the only part of my life that's fancy." Frankly, it made me itch. "It's one of the reasons I avoid this place as much as possible. Too much formality. I prefer my bar."

"It suits you better, Storm Bringer." She arched a brow.

"You heard that, huh?"

"Hard to miss."

I nodded and leaned back in my chair as the train rumbled away from the station. "When I was a teenager, I learned that I would grow into a magic I hadn't been born with. But then we learned my sister's prophecy."

She nodded encouragingly, and I told her more about the story of my sister. Of our flight from our Court and the years in hiding. At one point, Ryan brought food and drink, and Sora ate while I spoke.

When I finally finished the tale, she scrunched up her forehead. "So you have all this power you've never embraced."

"Essentially."

"I thought it was just more power like what you already have, but it's something different, isn't it?"

"Storms. Lighting, rain, the whole lot. Though I've never used it much. I gave it up right after I got it, pretty much."

"I can't imagine."

I shrugged. "It was easy. I had to protect my sister, so I couldn't become something that would draw attention. The Fae who hunted her is one of the most powerful Fae to ever live. Back then, if I'd I become the Storm Bringer, I'd have been equal to him. That gives me a fifty-fifty chance of defeating him. And if I didn't..."

"You wouldn't be around to protect your sister."

"And he would have found her. *I* would have led him to her." I took a sip of the beer that Ryan had brought me. "It was an easy decision."

"But now you can have it back."

"Now, I can. If I get there in time, and if I'm strong enough." I thought of the village that burned.

It was just a vision, wasn't it?

But why had that vision always accompanied the feeling of becoming the Storm Bringer again?

"Strong enough? I thought that ghostly lady said you were?"

"That was just to see if I was strong enough to retrieve the tools of the Rising One. We're going to Dartmoor to try to reach the Sacred Sea. It's heavily protected, and it'll be dangerous." Worry turned my stomach, and I reached for her hand. "Are you sure you want to do this?"

She scoffed. "You cannot be asking me that. Of course I do."

I frowned, then dug into my pocket for a transport stone. I pressed it into her hand. "If it gets too dangerous and I say to leave, you need to leave."

She hesitated.

"Vow it or I'm dropping you off at the nearest real train station to take you back to London."

She scowled. "Fine. I vow it."

Ryan appeared. "We've received permission to take you straight to the Dartmoor station. We'll be there in an hour."

"Thank you, Ryan."

He disappeared, and I stared at Sora. "So, you got any more secrets? You know all of mine."

"Fresh out, I'm afraid."

I grinned, then felt a stab of pain through my entire body. It took all I had not to double over at the table.

Sora frowned. "Are you all right?"

"Fine." My voice was rough as I dug into my pocket for a restorative draught. My vision blurred, and chills raced over my whole body. I should have had another hour before the weakness hit me.

I was running out of time faster than I'd expected.

My hands shook as I uncorked it, and I barely managed to drink it down before I collapsed. Immediately, strength rushed through my body, and I gasped. My vision cleared, and I found Sora kneeling by my chair.

"I can't believe you did this to yourself for me," she said.

"You didn't see what I saw." The memory of her falling was enough to chill my skin again. "And it's fate."

Just like she was my fated mate. Lucretia had sensed it. I knew it, too.

I just couldn't tell Sora yet. She wasn't Fae. And when you hadn't been raised with the concept of fated mates, it was kinda weird. Even creepy.

The idea that some unknown force in the universe had chosen a woman for me was weird as hell.

Except, now that I'd met her...

Fate had damned good taste.

"Come here. Don't sit on the ground." I helped her off the floor, pulling her onto the bench seat next to me. She cuddled against my side, and I wrapped an arm around her shoulders. Contentment filled me, a comfortable warmth that I hadn't expected.

"This is like a date," she said.

"I want a better one. Not that this isn't great, but I want a real one."

"Deal." She grinned, and the sight made something in my soul clutch.

We sat like that, resting and regaining our strength, and it was the best I'd felt in ages.

"We're nearly there." Ryan's voice shook me out of my stupor, and I looked up at him.

"Thanks, Ryan."

The kid nodded and turned to go. The train slowed as it neared the station. It was nearly dawn, but the moon was still out and bright enough to see by. The land outside began to look more alive—grass and gorse covering the hills of the moor.

"We've reached Dartmoor. The Fae live on another plane here, but their magic protects the place."

The train pulled to a stop at a tiny platform, and Sora and I went to the door. Ryan opened it, and we stepped out into the cool air. Claire would say it smelled like home, but it just smelled like nature to me. Potions & Pastilles was my home now.

A familiar figure waited for us at the other end of the platform, and I frowned. "Claire? How'd you know we'd arrive now?"

"Orion sensed you coming."

"Of course he did." I'd spent so much time with Orion as a kid that he had all but raised me, and I loved the old man like a father. Thanks to the sprites that considered him one of their own, he knew everything that happened on the moor.

Worry creased my sister's brow as she approached, her

brown hair blowing in the wind. She was dressed in her usual black leather fighting attire. "He says it's going to be dangerous, getting to the Sacred Sea."

"That's the point. Otherwise, the waters wouldn't be so valuable." I grinned at her, trying to reassure her.

She scowled at me. "I'm going to come with you and—"

The comms charm at my wrist buzzed, and the voice of my part-time staffer, Bridgette, echoed out. "Connor? I'm at P&P, working. There are some guys outside. Looking real creepy. Bald heads covered with tattoos, leather jackets. They came in and gave me a hard time. I got them to leave, but I think they're coming back."

Beside me, Sora stiffened. "They're there for me."

Claire's gaze moved to Sora. "Really?"

"What should I do?" Bridgette asked.

"My sister is coming," I said.

"Okay. Hurry."

I cut the connection on the comms charm and looked at Claire. "Will you go deal with them?"

She scowled at me. "Yes. But I want to help you with this if you need it, so call me."

"I promise."

She gave me a tight hug, then stepped back and drew a transport stone out of her pocket. "I'll see you soon."

She chucked the stone to the ground and disappeared.

Sora looked up at me, eyes worried. "Your sister can handle them?"

I chuckled. "Yeah. Without problem." Claire was insanely powerful.

Sora nodded, still looking concerned.

"Seriously, try not to worry." I dug into my pocket. "Normally, I wouldn't use a transport charm for such a short journey, but we're in a hurry."

Sora nodded and reached for my hand.

I gripped hers and threw the transport charm to the ground. A cloud of smoke burst up, glittering and bright. We stepped into it, and I imagined the portal in the human world that would lead to the Fire Fae realm. It was located near the middle of the moor.

The ether sucked us in and spun us through space, spitting us out in the middle of the wide-open landscape. Hills swept up in the distance around us, and we stood at the bank of a swiftly moving river. A clapper bridge stretched across it, the ancient stone slabs laid down thousands of years ago. There were many clapper bridges on the moor, but only this one provided access to the Fae realm. On the other side, a tiny forest of twisted oaks formed the portal that would lead us through.

"Ready?" I asked Sora.

"As I'll ever be."

12

Sora

Dartmoor was beautiful. For all the years that I'd lived in London, I'd never had a reason to come out here.

I should have.

There was a stark, barren beauty to this place of soaring hills and sweeping valleys. Massive stone pillars sat on top of each of the hills, looking like building blocks left behind by a forgetful god.

I pointed to them. "What are those?"

"Tors. They're made of granite and sit atop each of the hills." He pointed to another one, which was far bigger and located close, just on the other side of the river. "The Fire Fae palace is built onto that one. You'll see it when we cross over to their realm."

"And the humans have no idea the Fae are here." I

shook my head, marveling. "Just like Guild City, but in the countryside."

"The humans know nothing, but I think the sheep are onto us."

I laughed. "Which way?"

"We need to cross the bridge and enter the forest. From there, we'll be taken to the Fire Fae realm."

"Let's get to it, then." Worry tugged at me. There was no time to delay.

Connor led me over the bridge. On either side, crystal clear water rushed by. Dark stones were scattered on the bottom.

"Have you ever ridden rafts down this river? Fun ones, I mean. In a swimming costume. Maybe with a beer?" I asked.

Connor looked at me like I was insane, then laughed. "That's a good idea. That can be our first date."

"Pick a sunny day, and I'm there."

I had a feeling that it was probably pretty insane to ride rafts down a river through the Fire Fae kingdom, but I was glad that Connor went along with it. He didn't take himself too seriously, which I liked.

We reached the forest of tiny twisted oaks, and their magic swelled toward me, making me shiver. Each one was hardly taller than Connor, but they were thick with ancient growth, their limbs twisted and gnarled.

"These look like something out of a fairytale," I said.

"They're the oldest trees on Dartmoor. They grew small to withstand the wind."

He led me into the middle of the grove, and a heavy feeling of magic settled around me.

"Stand still and imagine your intentions toward the Fire Fae Court," he said.

"I have no intentions besides helping you."

"Then we'll have no trouble getting in."

We stood in silence as the trees reached their limbs out toward us. I had to resist a giggle as their branches tickled lightly against my skin. Magic flowed through me, and the ether sucked me in, dragging me through space. My head spun, and my vision blackened.

When my feet hit solid ground and I opened my eyes, almost everything looked entirely different. Oh, the landscape was the same, with the hills and valleys and tors. But now, there was a massive fiery castle sitting on top of the hill, built against the granite. It looked like it was made of glass that had been imbued with flame, and it was the most beautiful thing I'd ever seen. A long road led all the way up to the castle, and the village was built around it. Dozens of small houses lined the road, each made of the same material as the castle. They were gorgeous and ornate, and I was dying to get inside one and explore.

"To the castle?" I asked.

"No. Thank fates."

"You don't like the king and queen?"

"Loathe them."

It was the worst thing he'd ever said about anyone, actually. And I had a feeling he meant it. They'd evicted his sister from her home, after all.

"They're not outright evil," he said. "So don't worry about that. They mean the best for the kingdom. But they're myopic and don't always make the best decisions."

"Where are we headed, then?"

"There's an old Fae who helped me a lot when I was a kid. Our parents died early, and it was just us for the longest time. But Orion was like a father to me. He'll give us an update on the situation and help us get to the Sacred Sea more quickly."

"Does he live in one of the houses?" I spotted people walking around outside the homes, many of them tending to small gardens or children.

"He lives in a cottage on the other side of the hill," Connor said. "Not terribly fond of people."

"All right. Lead the way."

We walked away from the tiny forest and skirted around the hill. Though several people turned to look at us, they didn't wave. I eyed them as we walked and wondered about these people. The Fire Fae were strange, that was for sure. They'd been okay with the king and queen evicting poor Claire. Thank fates Connor had gone with her. I couldn't imagine what would have happened to me if I'd been evicted from Guild City as a kid.

He was a good man, Connor. I didn't know him well, but I was confident of that.

I was confident of a lot of things about him, actually.

Like the fact that he was the guy for me. In a forever way.

The thought nearly made me gasp aloud, but I knew it

like I knew my own name. I'd never had a seer's gift, but right now, I was seeing it so clearly that it had to be real. Connor and I were meant for each other. It was a strange connection—something I'd never felt before—but I could *definitely* feel it. Like I could feel the air in my lungs.

"We're nearly there." Connor's voice shook me from my thoughts, and I blushed.

He pointed to a small house that sat next to a twisted old tree at the base of the hill. Like the other houses, it appeared to be made of glass and flame.

An old Fae man sat on a chair under the tree, his clothing simple and his face lined. A smile stretched his lips, and he raised a hand to Connor.

I looked up to see Connor smile back, and there was pure joy in his expression. He waved to the man.

"Do you visit often?" I asked.

"No. Unfortunately not. I should, though."

"I imagine it was hard, back when you were evicted."

He nodded. "It was impossible. But I've seen him since then."

The man rose, and Connor picked up the pace. I quickened my steps to keep up, and we reached the old man. Connor hugged him, and they squeezed tightly.

"Caspian, my boy." The man grinned.

"Connor." His voice was gentle as he reminded the man.

"Of course, of course. Connor." The old man shook his head. "Can't say that I blame you."

"You always understood." There was appreciation in

Connor's voice. He gestured to me. "This is my friend, Sora."

"Friend, eh?" The old man's brows waggled a bit, and it was so ridiculous that I laughed. "I am Orion. Come, come. We will have some tea." The old man gestured us into the house, and we followed.

The interior was far larger than I'd expected, and the walls gleamed with a fainter glow within. It was a good thing, since the house was so brilliant on the outside that it'd be nearly impossible to keep your sanity if it was that bright on the inside—especially at night.

Orion led us to a small room, and we sat at a little table. He moved toward a doorway and looked behind him, "I'll be right back."

We sat, and I looked at Connor. "This feels like meeting your family."

"You are. Besides Claire, he is my family." He inclined his head, as if remembering something. "And I have some friends who are like family back in Magic's Bend. Cass is one of them. You'll meet the rest soon."

"Oh, I will, will I?" I grinned.

"If you want to."

"I do." This was moving fast. But hell, I *wanted* it to move fast. It just felt right.

Orion returned with the tea and set it on the table. He sat and passed the glasses around.

I picked up my glass and sipped, surprised at the bright burst of floral flavor. "It's lovely."

"My own blend." Orion's smile of pleasure faded as he

looked at Connor. "I know why you are here. Claire has visited."

"It's time."

Orion leaned forward. "I've readied mounts for you. And my sprites have provided some information about the Sacred Sea."

"I was hoping they would," Connor said.

"Not much gets past these ears, boy." Orion looked at me. "The sprites speak to me, bringing tales of what is happening on the moor. They are better company than all the people in the village combined."

I smiled at him.

"What can you tell us?" Connor asked.

Orion leaned forward. "As you know, the protections around the Sacred Sea are ever changing. My sprites suggest that the safest way to approach is to go via the River Dart, close to Dartmeet."

"Where the East Dart and West Dart meet?" Connor asked.

"Yes. Near the Clapper Bridge. Start there and follow the Dart downriver. You must follow the river closely to reach the Sacred Sea. Do not deviate from it, or you will become hopelessly lost, led astray by the wisps. Stay as close as you possibly can." His expression turned serious. "This is *vital*."

"How's the water level on the river?" Connor asked. "Is a boat possible?"

"No." Orion looked at me. "For your clarification, the Sacred Sea is not the ocean. It is a large lake, hidden deep within Dartmoor. No one approaches it unless the alternative is death."

I swallowed hard, hating the reminder. It was all a fun adventure until I remembered that part.

Orion harrumphed, then stood. "I will return shortly."

He moved slowly toward another room, and I whispered to Connor, "I like him."

"I think he likes you, too."

"How do you know?"

Orion returned before Connor could answer and set a bag down on the table. "Take this with you. When you reach the rock maze that surrounds the Sacred Sea, there is a tool inside that will help you find your way through. It's a lure that will call the sprites to you. They'll lead you." His gaze moved to me. "He's right. I do like you. You're smart and strong. And you're his fated mate."

"Fated what now?" I asked, surprise racing through me.

Connor dipped his head back and sighed, then looked at Orion. "Did now really seem like the best time? We're a bit busy."

"Fate waits for no one."

"That's the truth." Connor stood and looked at me. "I promise I'll tell you."

Every inch of my skin vibrated, and I stared at him. I didn't need that many explanations. *Fated mate* pretty much said it all right on the box, and I'd heard of it before.

I just hadn't expected to *be* one.

13

Connor

Sora was quiet as Orion led us out of his cottage, but I could feel her gaze on me.

How long have you known?

It had to be her first question, and I could feel it screaming through the air even though she was silent.

Gods, I hoped she didn't think I was a total creep.

"I have two ponies you can ride," Orion said. "They will help you get over Dead Man's Tor."

I dragged my attention from Sora toward Orion. "Thank you. That'll help immensely."

The Sacred Sea was so heavily protected that one couldn't just transport to the edge of it.

Orion led us to the side of his cottage, where two enormous ponies stood next to a tree, lazily chomping on grass.

Most Dartmoor ponies were tiny creatures, incapable of bearing a rider. But these two were gigantic by comparison, their shaggy black coats making them look almost fluffy.

"They just stay here?" Sora asked. "They don't wander the moor?"

"They are mine," Orion said. "Bred of magic and nature, which is why they are so large. They have the option to roam the moor, and they do. But Claire gave me enough warning that I could find them and call them back. They don't wear saddles, but if you hang on tight, they will take you where you need to go."

"It will be a huge help," I said. "The ground around Dead Man's Tor is so rocky and uneven—constantly shifting—that only ponies like this can safely navigate it. They know every inch of the moor."

Orion patted the side of one of the ponies. "These fellows are as reliable as the dawn."

The pony moved its huge head to nuzzle Orion's shoulder. The man looked positively diminutive next to the beast.

Orion stepped aside so that we could mount the ponies, and I stood next to one and gestured to Sora. "I'll help you up."

She nodded, her eyes wary. "I've never ridden a horse."

"City girl?"

"Born and bred."

"You'll be fine," Orion said. "These ponies know what they are doing. You just need to hang on."

"That's the part I'm worried about." Sora looked between the pony's back and the ground, and I knew what she was thinking: *That's a long way down.*

She wasn't wrong. But she also wasn't a wimp.

She strode toward me and put her foot into my cupped hands, then braced her hands on the pony's tall back. I boosted her up, and she swung a leg over the side, laughing with shock. She leaned forward and grabbed big handfuls of the pony's mane, and the creature barely shifted. "I think I can do this."

"I know you can." I mounted my own pony and nodded my thanks to Orion. "I'll be back to visit soon."

"See that you come more often. And just leave the ponies when you are done with them. They'll come back here on their own."

We said our goodbyes, and the ponies turned and trotted off across the moor.

"So...." Sora said, her brow raised.

"I suppose there are some things I didn't tell you." The wind blew as we rode, the ponies' strides eating up the ground as they headed to Dead Man's Tor.

"Yeah. Care to share?"

"The fated mate thing...I wasn't sure at first."

"And now you are?"

I shrugged, trying to play it cool.

She frowned, clearly not settling for that.

I was glad the pony knew where it was going, because it allowed me to focus on her. "Yeah. Yeah, I'm sure. But it doesn't mean you're obliged to feel anything, of course. It just means that fate thinks we're suited to each other."

She laughed wryly. "More suited to each other than to anyone else on the whole planet."

"Maybe." My voice turned intense. "But I'm not going to pursue you if you don't want it. I saw what that did to my sister, when her mate wouldn't stop coming for her. We had to hide for a decade."

Her eyes softened. "I didn't think you would."

I dragged a hand through my hair. "I like you, Sora. I'd like you even without the fated mate bond. And if you wanted to start with a date when this is all over—a real date—that'd be just about perfect, as far as I'm concerned."

She grinned. "I can do that."

Pleasure warmed my chest, but out of the corner of my eye, I caught a glimpse of Dead Man's Tor. We'd lost sight of Orion's cottage and the palace behind us, and the imposing obstacle of the rocky hill rose high ahead.

"That's Dead Man's Tor, isn't it?" Worry echoed in Sora's voice.

"It is." I pointed to the gray hillside that led up to the granite pillars on top. "The hillside is covered in rock instead of grass and gorse. It shifts constantly and is extremely dangerous. That's why we need the ponies."

As if they'd understood I was talking about them, they picked up the pace. Sora and I bent low over their necks, clinging tightly as they raced across the moor, leaping over thin streams that cut across the valley. We reached the hillside, and they began to climb, their hooves steady on the shifting rock.

Steadily, they ascended, strong and solid beneath us. The ground moved, cracking open in places as the piles of rocks shifted. Crevasses opened into the hill, dark fissures that looked endlessly deep. The ponies seemed able to anticipate the movement, shying out of the way right before we would have plummeted into the depths.

Higher and higher they climbed, moving faster as the ground broke open more and more.

We were nearly to the top when Sora screamed. I turned, spotting her pony teetering at the edge of a crevasse.

"Sora!"

Her pony leapt back, narrowly avoiding the drop.

"I'm fine!" Fear flickered in her eyes, but her spine was straight.

"We're almost there," I said. "Halfway. Hang on."

We reached the top of the tor, and the ponies skirted around the pillars of granite. The ride down the other side was a bit easier, but my heart thundered in my ears as I watched Sora's pony try to navigate the terrain.

By the time we reached the bottom of the hill, my skin was damp with sweat. "Are you all right?" I asked Sora.

"I'm just glad that is over." She looked ahead of us, searching the terrain of the valley.

There was a huge forest in the distance, and I pointed to it. "That's where we're headed. See the river that disappears inside the forest? That's the River Dart, our destination."

She nodded. "I see it."

The ponies carried us toward it, moving swiftly over the safer terrain of the valley. They leapt over the narrow creeks that turned it into a wetland, and eventually entered the forest. It was impossibly green there, with moss covering the ground and the canopy of leaves overhead. The sound of water rushing nearby drew my attention, and the ponies turned unerringly toward it.

The ponies approached the broad river and stopped next to the wide expanse. I spotted the clapper bridge to our left. It was far bigger than the one at the entrance to the Fae realm, the massive slabs of stone stacked on top of each other and rising out of the rushing river. Trees grew so close to the river on all sides that it would be impossible to ride alongside it.

I climbed off the pony and went to help Sora down. She swung her leg over the side of the horse, and my hands closed around her trim waist, lowering her to the ground.

"Thanks." She turned to the river. "We have to follow this?"

"Yes." I eyed the rocky river. The entire riverbed was made of small and large stones, the water crystal clear. "But the trees grow too close to the bank to walk alongside it."

Hundreds of trees lined the banks at uneven placement, their massive roots twisting around boulders and making it impassable. I looked at Sora. "If you don't mind me carrying you, I can try to fly us over it."

"Fine by me." She strode up to me, and I picked her up, one arm beneath her knees and the other behind her back.

Her warmth pressed against me, and I dragged my mind from inappropriate thoughts as I called on my wings.

It was only the second time I'd done it as an adult, and the sensation was still unfamiliar. They burst to life behind me, magically appearing through my clothes, and I launched myself in the air, clutching Sora close to my chest.

As I flew over the river, the trees shivered and moved. Their limbs reached out, and a branch coiled around my leg. It squeezed tightly, dragging me down.

"Shit." I fought it, straining my wings with all the power I had.

But the tree was too strong, magic sparking around the limb. No matter how hard I flew, the tree pulled harder.

I gave up, flying back to the ground to stand on the river's edge. I lowered Sora, and she stepped away.

"Well, that's not an option." I stared at the rushing river. The water moved fast, and the rocky bottom was uneven. "The river is too shallow in many places for a boat. We could try to walk through it, but it'll be slow and dangerous."

"Agreed. I don't like that option."

I turned to study our surroundings. There had to be a way to get there. The Sacred Sea was heavily protected but not impossible to reach. You had to earn your way there through smarts and strength.

I closed my eyes and reached out with my senses, trying to feel what type of magic was here. I could feel it sparking around the place—I just needed more info. "Do you feel the magic here?"

"Yes." Sora knelt and pressed her hand to one of the mossy boulders at the edge of the river. "Do you think there's some kind of hidden trigger that we can find that will reveal the way to follow the river?"

"Yes." The magic pulled harder from one direction, feeling almost familiar. Feeling almost like *my* magic, though I knew that had to be crazy.

I didn't open my eyes as I walked toward it, moving slowly to avoid tripping. I relied on my other senses, following the call of the spell. Fate had decreed that I would come here to finally embrace my magic, so I had to trust it.

"Are you on to something?" Sora asked.

"I think so." It pulled hard at me, a kind of familiarity leading me a few feet down the river's edge. I'd never had any kind of gift that would allow me to find things—not like my FireSoul friends did—but this was impossible to deny. It was like I'd been born to come here and find this.

Hell, maybe I had been.

Finally, I opened my eyes. My surroundings looked no different than they had—I stood at the edge of the river near a cluster of moss-covered boulders that were piled against the twisted roots of a tree trunk. I knelt, my hands going unerringly toward one of the larger boulders. I braced myself against it and shoved, heaving the enormous stone away from its resting place.

A small, dark crevice was revealed, and a flat stone rested within. It was dark with smeared dirt, and it called to me. I pressed my palm flat against it, feeling magic spark against my skin. It swirled around me, making my entire body vibrate. Golden sparkles flickered around my arm, rising up my body. It felt almost as if they were inspecting me to make sure I was the right person.

"Whoa," Sora said. "You're glowing."

I looked up and cracked a wry smile. "Guess this was meant to be."

The words were cheesy, but they were the only ones that fit.

Her gaze flicked toward the river. "Look!"

I turned, spotting the golden sparkles flying over the river, diving into the water and making it bubble and swirl. Large boulders rose to the surface, creating steppingstones through the rushing water.

"Holy fates, it worked!" Sora grinned widely at me.

"Looks like it did." The sparkles rushed down the river, dragging rocks up from the depths.

I withdrew my hand and watched as a path continued to rise through the surface of the water. I stood and approached the closest steppingstone. "Be alert as we go. I don't think this is going to be easy."

Sora nodded and moved beside me.

Tentatively, I put my foot on the steppingstone, gradually resting all of my weight on it. The boulder stayed strong, and I moved to the next one. Sora followed, and we began to travel down the river, jumping from stone to stone.

Magic sparked all around, and when the water splashed to my left, I looked down in time to spot a small creature reaching up from the depths. It was crystal clear, made entirely of water but shaped like a strange little man. It had a small head and two long, spindly arms. The creature grabbed my ankle and pulled hard.

I kicked it off, but another one jumped from my other side, leaping up and trying to grab me around the waist. It was the size of a small child, but impossibly strong as it gripped me. Pain flared as my ribs and lungs compressed.

I smashed my arm through the creature's body, and water droplets exploded everywhere, destroying the creature.

"What are these things?" Sora demanded, smacking a creature away as it leapt for her. Another lunged out of the water, headed straight for her.

She thrust out her hand, her magic flaring. A blast of gray smoke shot from her hand and enveloped the beast. It disappeared mid-leap.

"Some kind of water spirit." I called upon my shield from the ether and smashed it against a flying water creature, causing it to explode into thousands of water droplets. "Do you want a shield?"

Sora voided another. "I'm good. Let's keep going."

We raced across the steppingstones, smashing and

voiding the water creatures as they attacked. Water rushed around the boulders as we ran, shifting and moving to form the tiny attackers.

We ran, moving as quickly as we could while the beasts jumped toward us. Water exploded into thousands of droplets as I smashed the attackers.

"Do you feel that?" Sora asked.

I hadn't felt anything until she spoke, but then the threatening prickle of power came from behind. I turned back, spotting an enormous wave coming toward us—the river, giving chase.

"Go!" I shouted, grabbing her around the waist and swinging her onto the boulder in front of me so that I was between her and the wave.

She sprinted forward, leaping from steppingstone to steppingstone. Despite her shorter legs, she was fast and graceful. I sprinted after her, looking back to see the wave shifting and changing shape.

It morphed to form a four-legged beast with a huge head, like some kind of deformed southern Kelpie. I'd never seen anything like it. The creature was fast, galloping after us as more of the water surged behind it, rolling like a wave across the top of the river.

As I ran, I called my potion bag from the ether. I reached in, searching for anything that would slow the beast. Finally, my hand closed around a star-shaped bomb. I yanked it free and hurled it back at the Kelpie.

There was no hard surface for the glass to explode against. The potion bomb hit the creature's chest and absorbed. The attack seemed to enrage it, making it run faster after us, gaining with every step.

Shit.

I turned back and ran faster. "Keep moving! We may have to outrun it."

My lungs burned as I followed Sora, looking back to check on the beast that tracked us. It gained speed, closing the distance swiftly.

There would be no outrunning it.

My mind raced.

I had to keep it away from Sora. It could grab her and drown her.

It surged toward us, the water beast leading the massive wave behind it. I reached into my potion bag for one more bomb, finding it swiftly.

The creature was so close I could almost reach out and touch it. Instead, I drew a sword from the ether and turned to face it, praying Sora would keep going.

It loomed over me. I chucked the potion bomb up like it was a baseball and swung my sword like a bat, smashing the potion bomb right as the beast neared me. It exploded in a shimmer of cobalt liquid, spraying the water beast.

I ducked low, covering my head and praying that it worked.

14

Sora

I turned in time to see Connor use his sword as a bat. The glass potion bomb exploded against the beast's enormous, aqueous body, which looked like a semi-transparent, deformed horse.

Fear spiked through me, chilling my skin, as Connor ducked for cover.

As the potion splashed on the monster, it froze solid, turning to one huge block of ice. Behind it, most of the massive wave froze as well. The remaining water splashed into the river behind it.

"Holy fates." I bent low, gasping as I kept my eye on him. Shock raced through me. "I can't believe that worked."

He stood and dragged a hand through his dark hair. "Neither can I."

"You would have been dead."

"Maybe."

I had no idea what exactly that water demon could do, but I had a feeling that Connor would have been in a real bad state if it had gotten to him. Connor turned to inspect our surroundings, and I straightened. There was no time for freak-outs. We needed to keep moving and stay alert.

I peered into the water around my steppingstone, muscles tense, but none of the water sprites leapt out at me. Still shaking slightly, I turned to face downriver.

"Holy fates," I whispered in a rush.

The river sloped sharply downward into a valley, giving us a good view of what was to come. In the distance, the river led toward a sparkling lake. The trees that bordered the river disappeared, and soon, we'd be able to walk on the bank. Farther on, the river itself seemed to vanish beneath an expanse of enormous boulders that formed a protective circle around the water. That had to be the stone maze that Orion had mentioned, and the water must go underground before it reached the lake.

Connor joined me, stopping on the stone behind mine. "We're not that far away."

"I hope that whatever Orion gave us to help with the stone maze works, because it looks like it covers a lot of ground."

"It will be one of the last protections for the Sacred Sea, though. Once we get past it, we're almost there."

"It looks too small for a sea."

"Once you are close, the magic makes it much bigger. Like small houses that are enchanted to be larger on the inside."

I started forward, hopping from stone to stone. Together, we made our way along until the trees that lined the banks ceased and we were able to jump onto the grass. We followed the river toward the protective barrier of stones that surrounded the lake. We could no longer see the lake itself—just the towering granite that rose overhead. Up close, the rocks were much larger, at least fifteen feet tall and all jumbled on top of each other.

"Time to use the lure." Connor pulled his bag from the ether and removed the smaller bag that Orion had given him. He slipped the tiny silver lure free, and I could feel the magic of buzz through the air.

A low humming sounded in the distance, and I spun around to search for it. Tiny silver sprites zipped toward us. Shaped like miniature fairies, they glowed with an internal light that hummed a low, steady, oddly soothing tone. Four of them gathered in front of Connor, each no bigger than my palm. He held out the lure, allowing it to sit flat in his palm so that they could buzz around it.

The lure hummed a different tone, but it seemed to excite the sprites. They sang louder, zipping around.

"It's like Orion is sending them a message through the lure," I said.

"I think he is. I've never understood quite how they communicate, but this must be part of it."

The sprites began to drift away, heading toward the stone maze. We followed, keeping up easily. I had a feeling they could move a hell of a lot faster, but they were going slowly for us.

They led us toward a gap in the stone wall, and we followed them into the maze. The rock rose tall on either side of us, the passage narrow. Protective magic sparked all around, uncomfortable against my skin. I could feel it coming more strongly from the left, so I veered toward the right, sticking close to that side of the wall.

"The sprites will try to keep us from the dangers in the maze, but they aren't infallible," Connor said. "Stay wary."

I debated pulling my dagger from my pocket but left it there for now. Instead, I focused on my newly controllable void magic, elated that I could use it again without worrying I'd knock myself out.

The sprites zipped left and right, ignoring some passages through the maze and taking us through others. At one point, the protective magic vibrated so strongly against my skin that my stomach turned.

In front of me, Connor's hands twitched, as if he were ready to draw something from the ether, but he just wasn't sure what.

When an enormous pillar to our left rocked in place, threatening to fall right on us, he lunged backward and shoved me out of the way. He fell on top of me, covering me with his body. The rock crashed to the ground, landing with a hard thud that seemed to shake the stone walls around us.

Connor was warm and strong as he leaned over me, his face close to mine, worry gleaming in his eyes. "Are you all right?"

I nodded. "Yeah. Yeah, I'm fine."

"Your heart is thundering so loudly I can hear it."

I laughed. "I think you hear your own heart."

"Maybe." His eyes dropped to my lips and warmed.

Would he kiss me?

Before he could, a sprite appeared near our heads, zipping left and right in an agitated manner.

Connor's jaw firmed. "We need to go. This does not count as me keeping my guard up."

I cracked a weak smile. "No kidding."

He stood, and I followed. The huge pillar lay across the path at an angle, leaving a small spot for us to crawl beneath, and the sprites zipped through. Connor crouched low and passed through quickly. I followed, feeling a hell of a lot less graceful as the mud stuck to my hands and knees.

We climbed out on the other side, and I paused next to Connor, trying to brush the mud off me. The sprites flew on, and we followed. Four more boulders fell in our way, but we were quick enough to avoid them. My heart was going a mile a minute by the time we saw the light at the end of the stone maze.

"Thank fates," Connor murmured.

We strode toward it, and the magic of the Sacred Sea filled the air. It felt welcoming and repelling all at one, a strange sensation that made my stomach turn.

We reached the very end of the maze, and the sprites flew straight up toward the sky, disappearing.

I stood next to Connor, peering out at the lake. The shore was about a hundred yards from us—impossibly far away and yet so close. It gleamed a dark navy, the surface glittering under the light of the sun.

"It's freaking huge," I said.

"That's the spell."

I whistled low under my breath. "Some spell." It was *way* bigger than it'd looked before. "What now?"

Connor shifted, looking around. "This will be the dangerous bit. The waters of the Sacred Sea are one of the most powerful potion ingredients in the world. Serious magic protects it. I need to get past that magic and get some of the water to make my potion."

"Then we get out of here and head back to your workshop?"

He shook his head. "I need to make the potion here. The magic in the water has a half-life of only a few minutes."

"Crap. So it's basically useless if you don't use it right away?"

"Exactly. I'll combine it with my blood and the other ingredients, and if the tools of the Rising One are as powerful as they are supposed to be, I should be fixed up within minutes."

I nodded, staring around at the empty stretch of grass between us and the lake. The protective magic was fierce, and I wondered what would be waiting for us.

I flexed my fingers, ready to zap it into oblivion. "I've got your back."

He squeezed my arm, looking down to meet my face. "I've known you for barely a day—how are you so good to me?"

"You got me my magic back, dummy." I raised my hand and wiggled my fingers, as if to indicate the power I now had. "And I like you."

"I don't deserve you."

"You don't have me yet." I grinned, then stood up on my toes and pressed a quick kiss to his lips. He groaned low in his throat, and I could feel his fingertips press briefly to my sides before disappearing. It was as if he wanted to clutch me to him but resisted.

I savored the last of the kiss and pulled away, looking up to meet his eyes. "But I'll be wanting that date if we get through this."

"We'll get through this." He squeezed my arm. "But you need to use that transport charm to get out of here if things get dangerous. I'll follow."

"Sure." I smiled and nodded, knowing there was no way in hell I'd ditch him.

"I mean it, Sora. I can see you don't intend to do it. But if the time comes, you have to."

I scowled at him. "You can't tell me what to do." My frown morphed to a grin. "Anyway, we're here, aren't we? There's nowhere to go but forward."

Frustration seemed to seep from his pores, but the

slight twist of his lips looked almost like a smile. "Stay safe. It's the most important thing to me."

His voice was so serious that a shiver went through me. I nodded. "You, too."

We turned to stare out at the lake. After a minute, he asked, "Ready?"

"Yeah." I stepped forward.

Together, we ran for the shore. It took only a moment before the rock wall surrounding us began to move. It shifted, boulders tearing away from the wall and rolling toward us. They were massive, most of them the size of cars. And fast. Damn it, they were as fast as cars, too.

Connor drew his potion bag from the ether and reached in, pulling out a red glass ball. He chucked it at one of the nearest boulders, and the glass orb exploded against the side. Red liquid splashed, and the rock disintegrated on the spot.

But there were so many. I called upon my magic, hurling a blast of gray void smoke at a boulder that was about to knock me over. It slammed into the rock, sucking it away into space.

"Go!" I shouted. "I'll cover you!"

"Get out of here if it's too dangerous!" he yelled back.

"Okay, I promise." I knew they were the words he needed to hear, even as I was unsure of their truth.

He sprinted for the lake, and I got between him and the attacking rocks. They rolled toward us, leaving deep dents in the earth as they moved.

My magic flowed strong as I called it to the surface and hurled it at the boulders. The smoke flew fast, the boulders disappeared, and confidence soared through me. I felt complete for the first time in years.

15

Connor

I sprinted toward the edge of the Sacred Sea, hating to leave Sora to guard my back. But those rocks would keep coming, and we needed to be quick.

And she was insanely powerful. I didn't need to worry about her as much as I did.

One of the boulders hurtled toward me, and I threw a disintegration bomb at it, causing it to collapse into dust. Quickly, I turned to see Sora void three massive rocks. A huge smile stretched across her face, and her eyes glinted with concentration. She'd never looked so beautiful.

My heart thundered as I raced toward the sea, the magic calling to me. I blasted two more rocks with potion bombs before reaching the shore. As soon as I neared it, I stashed my potion bag back in the ether. I needed to be quick here.

I pulled a second bag from the ether and withdrew the tools of the Rising One. The tiny cauldron glinted gold under the sunlight, and the blade looked sharp. Magic sparked from the tools, making my fingertips buzz. Finally, I removed the small vials of ingredients. There were only two—Esphoria and Wisloram, two common Fae herbs—and I measured them quickly. I'd had this potion memorized for years, and it came easily.

Out of the corner of my eye, I could see Sora destroying the rocks that hurtled at me, zapping them into oblivion with her magic.

Quickly, I sliced into my wrist, letting my blood drip in a crimson stream into the cauldron. When enough had filled the vessel, I picked up a small ladle.

Anticipation thundered through me as I moved to dip it into the lake. The water gleamed invitingly. As the ladle neared the surface, it became more difficult to move. It felt almost like the air was made of Jell-O that grew more and more solid as I neared the surface.

"You think to take the waters of the Sacred Sea without earning them?" The feminine voice vibrated with power, and I looked up, shocked.

A figure was rising from the depths, her form glittering like the sun. She had no easily discernible features, but the magic that vibrated from her was strong. "Storm Bringer, you are here to face your fate."

"I am." Slowly, I rose. "But who are you?"

She gestured to the shimmering water behind her, her movements graceful. "I am the guardian of the Sacred Sea, the source of its power and magic."

"How do I earn the right to take some of the water?"

It was impossible to make out her features, but it looked almost like she smiled. "I am glad to see that you are asking the correct questions."

"I try." I pointed back to Sora, who was still fighting off the boulders. Worry for her tightened every muscle in my body, but I tried not to let it show. "Any chance you could call those boulders off?"

"No."

"Then could I do whatever is necessary quickly? I care about her, and she won't leave me, even if I insist."

"You know her well."

"Well enough, and I don't want her hurt. What do I need to do?"

"Prove yourself. I will allow you to take a ladle of the water and create your potion. Your magic will return to your wings and complete you, but you won't be able to keep it. Not unless you earn it."

"How do I do that? And how long do I have?"

"Hours, perhaps minutes." Slowly, she began to drift back to the sea. "It all depends on you."

I reached out. "Stop, please."

She hesitated, head tilted.

"I've been around enough godly beings to know that there can be rules. Unexpected ones."

She laughed, and the sound was eerie against the noise

of Sora keeping the boulders from crushing me. "You are a clever one, Connor."

"You won't tell me how I must prove myself, but is anything off limits in the process? Can I have help?"

"From the woman behind you?"

"From her. Or anyone else." I'd never been at a big battle that wasn't solved by more than one person. No matter how powerful the person, life had taught me that we were all better as a team.

"Anyone may help you." She inclined her head, and I was almost certain that it was a gesture of respect. "After all, one of your most admirable qualities is your ability to gain allies."

I wasn't sure I'd call my friends allies. My life was hardly a war zone, no matter what it looked like at the moment. But I wasn't going to correct her.

"Thank you," I said.

She nodded one last time, then drifted back to the water. Before she descended into the depths, she looked at Sora and murmured, "You've finally found her. Shame you'll have to choose."

Confusion shot through me, but she was gone.

Quickly, I knelt and picked up the ladle, dipping it into the shimmering water. It went easily this time, and I added it to the tiny golden cauldron.

Immediately, the mixture inside began to bubble and steam, despite the lack of a heat source. I looked back to check on Sora, spotting her racing across the grass behind me, shooting her blasts of gray magic at the boulders that kept trying to reach me. They disappeared, one after the other, but there were so many of them.

I turned back to the tiny cauldron and muttered, "Come on, come on."

From behind me, a scream sounded. I whirled around, finding Sora on the ground. One of the boulders had plowed into her, and the others were coming. She tried to scramble to her feet, but her leg appeared broken.

At my side, the cauldron continued to bubble.

Shame you'll have to choose.

The goddess's words echoed in my head. Was this what she had meant? I'd have to choose between the potion that would save me and saving Sora?

It was no choice at all.

I called upon my wings. They came quickly, though I could feel that they weren't right. It felt as if they were weaker. But they were still there, and they would work. They had to.

I launched myself into the air, spinning so that I could see Sora. A half dozen boulders hurtled for her, each the size of a car. They moved so fast that she didn't stand a chance—especially on the ground.

She hit one with a void blast, then another. They both disappeared, but the last four were nearly to her. I shot toward her, my wings carrying me fast through the air. Fear iced my spine. She blasted one, then another.

The last two were only feet from her when I swooped down and grabbed her, yanking her into my arms. I shot upward, desperate to get her away from them.

She screamed, a sound of pain that tore at my heart.

"I've got you." I tried not to jostle her leg as I flew her toward the top of the stone maze that surrounded the Sacred Sea. The maze still sparked with dangerous magic, and I knew we couldn't fly over it.

I reached the tops of the huge boulders that formed the maze and gently laid her down on it.

"Connor." She gripped my arms and stared at me, fear in her eyes. "Did you not finish the potion?"

"I will." I fumbled for the potion bag that I kept stored in the ether. "Where are you hurt?"

"My leg." She winced, her face pale. "The boulder crushed it."

Finally, I found the healing potion. It was my most powerful, and should knit her back together in no time. I uncorked it and handed it to her. "Drink this."

She took it without question and gulped it. I watched, anxious, praying that it would work as well as I knew it could. Quickly, the color returned to her cheeks, and the pinched skin around her eyes smoothed. "Holy fates, that feels better."

My shoulders relaxed, and I retracted my wings.

Her gaze moved to the sacred sea, and a frown creased her brow. "Connor. How are you going to get there?"

I turned to look at the sacred sea. The rolling boulders were gone, replaced by an army of stone soldiers. Half carried enormous swords, and the other half were armed with some kind of crossbows that could shoot me right out of the sky.

Fates, that guardian was determined to make me work for it.

"Where are we?" My sister's voice echoed from behind me, and I turned in surprise.

She and Cass stood on top of the rock walls that created the stone maze, only ten feet from us. Each was dressed in their fight-wear—Claire in black leather and Cass in jeans and her beaten leather jacket.

Slowly, I stood, helping Sora to her feet. "How did you get here?"

Claire looked toward me. "Some lady who was made of water appeared to me when Cass and I were having drinks. She said you needed me."

"And I came along." Cass's eyes shined with interest. "She glittered like diamonds."

I looked back to the Sacred Sea, remembering my question for the guardian.

She was giving me another chance.

I'd chosen Sora over the potion that would save me—something I'd do again in a heartbeat—but she was giving me another chance. With backup.

"He needs to get to the shore," Sora said. "And we have to buy him time to make the potion."

"We can do that," Claire said.

Cass looked at Sora. "You're a void mage?"

"Yep."

Cass grinned and cracked her knuckles. "That will be fun."

Cass was a Mirror Mage, able to mimic the power of

any nearby supernatural. Apparently, she was planning to try Sora's gift on for size.

"Go, brother," Claire said. "We've got your back."

"You always do."

"After years of you having ours, I'd say it's only fair," Cass said.

I nodded at them. "Stay safe." I turned to Sora, then pulled her toward me and pressed a kiss to her lips. "You, too."

I could feel Claire's wide eyes on me as I pulled back, but I ignored her gaze.

She said nothing as she strode up to the edge of the stone, overlooking the expanse of land between us and the edge of the Sacred Sea.

Sora

Connor's sister stood at the edge of the stone wall, overlooking the horde of monsters between us and our goal. There were more than a hundred of them, and we'd have to be clever if we wanted to beat them. Ebony wings flared from Claire's back, and she launched herself into the air.

A dozen stone soldiers turned their crossbows toward her, firing in unison. Huge iron spikes shot through the air, headed right toward her. Her hair blew on the wind as she threw out her hand. Magic sparked as a shield of light formed between her and the projectiles. It was so bright it nearly blinded me, and I only caught glimpses of the projectiles bouncing off the shield. More flew, coming from all angles, and she darted for the ground.

She landed right in front of us and looked up. "You take them out, and I'll cover for you!" She directed the shield of light ahead of her, where it created a barrier about ten feet tall by ten feet wide.

Connor drew his potion bag from the ether and strapped it over his chest before leaping down behind her. He reached inside for a bomb, then hurled it at a stone soldier who approached from the side. The bomb splashed against the creature's chest, and it exploded into dust.

Cass and I jumped down beside Claire and Connor. Claire started forward, forcing her light shield ahead of us, clearing a path through the defending stone soldiers.

They flowed around the side of her shield, but we were ready for them. I couldn't feel Cass mimicking my magic, but the red-haired mage was able to easily throw blasts of gray void smoke at any creature who came too close.

I did the same, taking them out, one after the other. Connor defended the back side of our little group, hurling potion bomb after potion bomb. Every single one was immensely effective, destroying its target in seconds.

My heart raced as we fought, and my magic began to grow weaker. We were using so much of it.

I drew my dagger from my pocket, feeling the magic prickle around the hilt.

Grow.

The blade responded to my thought, lengthening into a massive sword. A stone monster darted for me, and I swiped out with the blade, going for the creature's left leg, hoping to topple it to the ground.

The blade slammed into the beast's stone limb, and it tottered, collapsing onto its side with a crash.

The monsters were too close for Connor's potion bombs, so he drew a huge ax from the ether.

"You had that stored in there?" I shouted, disbelieving.

"Gotta be prepared." He grinned at me, then swung the ax at the nearest attacker.

It crashed into the beast, shattering it into a dozen pieces. Connor moved fast, fueled by immense strength. His ax smashed into one monster after another, leaving a trail of broken rock in our wake.

I alternated between my void magic and my sword, using the blade opportunistically, trying to time it with when I could take the easiest shot at a leg or an arm.

Fighting like this wasn't my specialty, but Connor had my back, taking out the stone soldiers before they could land a blow. Behind me, Cass kept up the onslaught of void magic, eliminating one monster after another. She seemed to have an endless well of magical power, and Claire was no slouch, either. Her light shield kept us protected from the front, cutting our way through the crowd.

"Nearly there!" Connor shouted.

Thank fates, he was right.

The shield of Claire's magic was blinding, but around

the edges, I could spot the glittering of the water. My lungs were burning and my muscles aching, but at least we were almost there.

"Shifting right!" Claire moved the shield to the right, and we rotated, forming a barrier between us and the edge of the Sacred Sea.

"Go!" I said to Connor. "We've got your back."

16

CONNOR

Sora, Claire, and Cass stood watch behind me as I moved to the edge of the Sacred Sea. Claire had gotten us right up to the edge where my cauldron and tools still sat. In an act of divine fate, none of the tools had been broken.

I knelt, working quickly. The cauldron was still steaming, but the bubbles had slowed, revealing a pale blue potion. It was still good, though barely. If the steam were gone entirely, it'd be worthless.

I lifted it to my lips and chugged it down quickly.

Immediately, my head began to spin. The world around me blurred as pain streaked through my body. Sweat popped to my skin, making me hot and cold at once. Magic swirled through me, seeming to come from the air itself, filling me with a rush. Power raced through my veins, surging toward my back.

My wings, which I'd stored away, burst forth. They felt different—complete, stronger. No longer a drain on the rest of me. The magic that sparked through me swirled on the air, surrounding me with bright white sparkles. Lightning seemed to shoot through my veins, and all I could smell was the scent of an oncoming rainstorm.

Time seemed to slow, the world around me coming to an abrupt halt.

Suddenly, I was no longer in the present. My hands and arms had grown skinnier, my thighs as well. A battered silver bracelet was attached to my wrist.

Holy fates, I hadn't seen that bracelet in years.

My arms flickered, going from skinny to muscular in front of my eyes.

I was in the past—or maybe I was just remembering it, I wasn't sure. I turned around, spotting Sora and the others who surrounded me. They looked frozen in time, their bodies stuck in defensive poses as they shot magic at the stone soldiers who tried to attack. The soldiers were frozen as well, thank fates.

Lighting streaked through the sky overhead, making the day blindingly bright. Thunder cracked, and I would have jumped if I hadn't expected it.

But I did expect it.

The last time I'd worn this bracelet, I'd been a teenager who'd first received this magic while kneeling by the River Dart.

A second bolt of lightning lit the sky, slamming into my body. Pain roared through me. Agony blurred my vision as I watched the silver bracelet melt off my wrist, gone forever.

The lightning raced through my body, stiffening my limbs and making me feel like I could fly apart, breaking into a million pieces.

Magic and lightning twisted through my bones and muscles, filling me with strength and power, just like it had the first time. Through the pain, I felt it fill my wings and knit me back together, making me whole.

Behind me, my allies were still frozen. Ahead of me, the Sacred Sea called. Visions of the dream that had haunted me flickered in my mind's eye—the burning village. It called so strongly that it felt like a hook had lodged in my heart and pulled me forward, toward the sea.

Why now?

It yanked, pulling on me.

The water of the Sacred Sea glittered dangerously, suggesting that death and danger waited ahead. Wading into an endless sea, armed only with wings and lightning, was a recipe for disaster. But it pulled on me, visions of the dream flashing in my head. Flames, drought, people dying. It pulled and pulled.

They needed me.

I didn't know how I knew it, or who they were, but I knew it like I knew my own name. Like I'd been born for this.

Hell, maybe I had. I'd been having dreams of these people my whole life.

I rose, not hesitating as I strode into the water. The cold lake soaked into my boots as I walked, rising to my knees, hips, thighs. I moved faster, charging into the sea. Ancient knowledge pulled on me, something I couldn't describe for all the power in the world.

As the water closed over my head, calmness suffused me, followed quickly by darkness as the ether sucked me in and spun me through space.

Moments later, I appeared in a new place—one that was terribly familiar yet extremely strange. My wings caught the air. It was so much easier to use them now—ten times more natural than it had been when I'd first grown them in the Sorcerer's Guild. I hovered over the village, seeing it as I'd seen it so many times before.

The day had turned to dusk, and a blazing red sun crept toward the horizon. Below me, a valley spread out. In the center, a small village.

All around, the land was parched and dry. The grass had died in favor of dirt, and the entire place looked like it was covered in dust.

Many of the people in the village had wings, but they drooped with weakness and defeat. They were Fae, like I'd expected, though I had no idea which kind. They were familiar, all the same, as if they'd been with me my whole life. In a way, they had.

In the distance, I caught sight of a gleaming white figure.

The guardian of the Sacred Sea.

I ignored her in favor of studying the scene below me. I had to help these people. For so long, I'd thought they were just a figment of my dreams. But no. Now that I was here, I knew. They were my fate. I'd been seeing them for years because I was meant to help them.

I flew over the village, my wings strong and healthy. In the distance, flames flickered. A long-dead forest was burning, the red tongues of fire flicking upward. It spread fast, reaching toward the village. The ground was covered in so much dead grass that the blaze could travel to the village if the winds were right.

The winds would be right.

I'd been fated for this. It was half the reason I had these damned powers, anyway. The guardian of the Sacred Sea knew it, and now I knew it, too.

I circled the village, my heart pounding in my ears. In the distance, the fire raced closer. I could smell the smoke and burning brush as it roared across the landscape.

I called on my magic, a power that I'd barely had a chance to practice with when I'd first gotten it as a teenager. It came easily, the lightning bursting to life inside me. I shoved it aside in favor of rain, calling upon the moisture that would drown out the fire.

The sky turned dark, and rain began to fall. Heavy, wet droplets suppressed the flames, making steam fill the air. But the blaze was too strong. It continued to roar, creeping across the land toward the village.

The people screamed, and my heart clutched.

This wasn't enough.

They'd suffered so long under the drought. Their misery had fueled my dreams for years, so strong and powerful I could feel it as my own. And now the fire was going to finish the job, snuffing out their village.

This was more than just a matter of calling on the elements and creating a storm. But I kept the rain coming, feeling like it was flowing from my soul and onto the flames. They were unnaturally strong, the product of a curse. Only magic could keep them going in the face of my power. As the rain poured, I flew over the village, searching for any sort of clue. There had to be *something*.

The ground itself seemed to be shimmering with dark smoke. It'd been hard to see at first, with the blazing red sun turning the entire landscape to shades of crimson and orange. The dark mist crept along the ground, thicker in some areas than it was in others. If I focused on it, I could feel the evil of the magic.

Someone had cursed this land long ago. The magic had the stale feel of age, but it was unmistakable. I followed the feeling around to the other side of the village, finding an area where the smoke was darkest.

Right next to an old well.

The tiny structure sat apart from the village, ancient and forgotten—a remnant of their past. But I could feel the darkness within it.

I flew down, landing on the muddy ground. It sloshed around my feet. If I wasn't quick, I would flood this place while trying to keep it from burning.

I strode toward the well, finding the shaft entirely filled in. Dirt had been packed into the hole, and dead grass now covered the top.

The dark magic pulsed from deep within, coming from somewhere in the earth.

Shit.

Whatever power was cursing this land was so far underground that I wouldn't be able to reach it.

No.

I dragged my hands through my hair. There had to be a way.

Lightning crackled in my veins.

An idea flared. It seemed impossible, but I had to try. If there was any water left in the well at all, I might be able to blast the whole thing open to get to the curse inside.

Anyway, there were no other options. I had to be strong enough, because there was no way I could get digging machinery out here. That was ridiculous.

I called upon the lightning within me, drawing it from the sky. I directed my hand toward the well, blasting it as thunder cracked. The bolt struck so hard and so fierce that the earth exploded upward. Steam billowed.

Thank fates.

I called upon more lightning, hitting it again. The bolt was so strong that it struck deep into the earth, boiling the water in the well and causing the ground to explode. I gave it all the power I had, grateful for the combination of science and magic that blew the well apart.

The darkness still called from deep within, and in the

distance, the flames roared. I could hear the screams of the Fae as they tried to evacuate their homes.

I launched myself into the air to get a better vantage point, shooting more lightning into the well. It plowed deeper, causing explosions that dug deep down into the earth.

There was so much steam filling the sky that it was nearly impossible to see, but I felt it. It hit me like a blow to the face when my lightning blasted away the last of the earth between myself and whatever was cursing this land.

I flew downward, squinting against the burning steam that billowed out of the well. As the steam dissipated, the shaft loomed dark and deep, the magic within it as evil as anything I'd ever felt…yet familiar. Far too familiar, thanks to my dreams.

A calming sense of fate suffused me as I flew down into the darkness. It was damp and warm, so black that it was nearly impossible to see. If it weren't for the glowing green light at the bottom, I wouldn't be able to see at all.

The magic that emanated from it made my stomach turn and my skin chill. Someone had put this down here long ago, and it had come to life, the magic seeping through the ground and bringing the drought that had nearly destroyed this place. I'd heard of curses like this, but I'd never seen one.

I landed near the small green stone that pulsed with evil magic. The bottom of the well shaft was only about four feet in diameter, and the water in it turned the bottom to mud.

The gem called to me, and I bent low, about to pick it up.

No.

It was too dangerous. Knowledge pulsed within me, and I closed my hand into a fist.

I couldn't touch it, but I had to destroy it.

There was only one option. I called upon the lightning within me once again, feeling it burn and crackle in my veins. I drew it down from the sky, hearing the crack of thunder as it shot into the well shaft and pierced the green stone.

The dark magic within it pulsed, resisting.

I hit it again, calling on an even bigger burst of lightning.

Again, the cursed stone resisted.

I gave it everything I had, knowing that I was permanently sacrificing some of my power.

The lightning bolt that shot down through the well shaft was so huge that it struck me as well. Pain flared, tearing through my muscles as the lightning enveloped both me and the stone.

For the briefest moment, I could feel the curse's dark magic seep inside of me. It seemed to suck all the magic out of me, forcing a drought inside my body that made me as powerless as a human.

Then it burst outward, the curse evaporating on the air as my magic overpowered it.

I collapsed to my knees in the darkness, the magic fading in the air around me. Panting, my shoulders bent, I tried to get my strength back.

Was all of my magic gone?

I'd known it was a risk when I'd done it. I'd gotten my magic back, yet so quickly I might have lost it.

Memories of the burning village filtered through my mind.

Worth it.

That vision had haunted me most of my life, and now it was done. The worst had come to pass—it was true—but now it was over.

I drew in a shuddering breath and stood. The sky above blazed red with the light of the setting sun. It was a long way up to the surface.

Aching, I called upon my wings, grateful to find that they still worked. Magic still pulsed through my veins, too, growing stronger with each moment.

I launched myself into the air, reaching the surface only a few seconds later. The wind chilled my skin as I flew higher, observing the scene.

The rain still fell, but it was natural this time. The curse that had forced the drought was gone, and this place could take care of itself.

In the distance, the gleaming form of the guardian of the Sacred Sea hovered in the air. She drifted toward me. I waited, watching as she approached.

I could feel the magic still in me—possibly weaker than it had been, but there. I could call on the rain if I needed to, on the lighting or wind.

She stopped in front of me and inclined her head. "You

did well."

I looked at the scene beyond her. "I always thought it was just a dream."

She shook her head. "It was your fate, waiting for you."

"What if I had never gotten my magic back?"

She shrugged. "They would have died."

I watched the people in the village below. They celebrated the rain that finally fell from the sky. "Who cursed them?"

"I do not know, but it happened long ago. Long before you were born."

"Was I born to save them?" My sister had been born to save our people, the Fire Fae. Had I been born to save these unknown others?

"Perhaps."

"But I don't know them."

"Do you need to?"

"No." The answer came easily. All I needed to know was that they were in trouble and I could help.

"Well, there's your answer. You'll help where you can and when you can with the magic that you gave up for your sister."

The mention of her reminded me of the situation I'd left them in. "Can I go back to them? They're in danger."

The guardian nodded. "I'd say that you can. And may fate's best wishes be upon you."

I'd never heard the saying before, but I nodded. "Thank you."

She flicked her hand, and the ether sucked me in spinning me through space.

When the world stopped whirling, I found myself kneeling at the shore of the Sacred Sea once more. I surged to my feet and spun around.

Time seemed to start again. Sora, Claire, and Cass unfroze, bursting to life as the fight continued. I stepped in front of them and threw out my hands. A hundred bolts of crackling lighting shot from my palms, blasting into the stone soldiers as thunder cracked deafeningly through the air.

The soldiers stopped, toppling to the ground and becoming unassuming piles of rocks.

"Whoa," Claire's voice sounded. "That is a badass power."

I turned to face them. Sora looked at me. A huge grin stretched across her beautiful face as she spotted me. "Connor! You're fixed!"

"I think I am."

"I'd say you are," Cass said. "You just took out a hundred stone soldiers in one fell swoop."

I could still feel that I'd lost some of my new power when I'd stopped the curse that had almost destroyed that village, but it had been worth it.

All around, the day was silent. The stones lay scattered on the ground, the magic fallen still.

My sister met my gaze, a million questions in her eyes. "You have some stories to tell, I think."

17

S̲ora̲

Twelve hours later, I snoozed in a chair that had been pulled up to the door of Connor's lab. It didn't fit all the way in, so I was halfway in the narrow kitchen, but I didn't mind. He'd been hard at work these last hours, trying to make the potion that we'd give to the Devil of Darkvale. After everything that had happened, I couldn't believe we were almost done.

But we were. He'd told Claire everything he'd been hiding all these years—she'd been shocked, of course, but she'd understood—then he'd gotten to work on the potion. After Connor and I had told her the truth, Claire and I had spent some time getting to know each other.

I really liked her. And Cass.

In fact, I really liked this whole place.

As I watched Connor, I wondered where my life would go.

I had options. We'd come so close to death that I'd realized maybe what I was doing wasn't really *living*. I could do better.

I settled deeper into the chair. Music echoed through the kitchen, something I didn't recognize, but Connor hummed along to as he worked.

"How is it coming?" I asked.

"Almost there." He shot me a grin over his shoulder. "Getting angsty?"

"Ready to have the Devil off my back and go on that date with you."

He grinned. "In that case, I'll hurry up."

I laughed and watched him work. Finally, he turned, a glass vial in his hand. "Ready?"

I hopped upright. "Am I ever."

"Let's go."

"Let's? Don't you mean *me*?"

"No. I'm going with you."

"The Devil won't let you in."

"I'd like to see him try to keep me out."

Warmth flowed through me. I didn't want to put Connor in yet another dangerous position, but after what I'd seen of him these last couple days, I knew he could handle himself—even with the Devil. And if I were being honest, I was damned glad to have him at my back. "Okay. Thanks."

He grinned. "Let's get a move on."

We went directly to London using one of Connor's transport stones. The midafternoon sun was surprisingly bright, welcoming us to the dreary alley where the Haunted Hound was located.

We slipped through the alley and into the pub. Mac no longer worked the bar and had been replaced with a guy I didn't know well. He ignored us as we went to the secret entrance to Guild City.

Connor moved quickly, as if he knew exactly where he was going and was ready to get the job done—which, I supposed, was exactly the case. He led us through the wall, and then through the gate into Guild City, which was busier than it had been the first time we'd come. The lunch crowd was out in force, filling the bars and restaurants on the square.

Connor turned to me. "Care to lead the way?"

I nodded, my heart thundering. I wasn't afraid so much as anxious to have this over with. I'd seen how Connor had blasted a hundred soldiers in one go. Even the Devil of Darkvale couldn't fight that.

And he no longer held my home over my head.

As much as I loved this place—what wasn't there to love?—I'd seen more of the world now. There were more places I could be happy. More people I could be happy with. Which meant that even if the Devil wasn't satisfied with the potion we'd made for him, he could kick me out, and it wouldn't devastate me.

Confidence filled me as I strode down the street. This was the first time in years I'd walked through Guild City with my magic intact. I was as powerful as anyone here, no longer a second-class citizen who was as likely to blow myself up as I was to use my magic properly.

It didn't take long to reach the Devil's place, and the bouncers at the door seemed to recognize me immediately. Both were bald and wore identical suits. They hesitated at the sight of Connor, who stuck close to my side as we waited.

The one on the right spoke briefly into the comms charm on his wrist, then nodded at us and opened the door. A tall, slender hostess led us through the beautifully appointed nightclub and toward the back.

We stopped at the big black door that led to the Devil's office.

"Don't worry," Connor murmured at me. "I've got your back."

I grinned at him and squeezed his hand. "I know."

When the door swung open to reveal the Devil seated at his desk, I realized that he looked slightly...shocked.

Perhaps *shocked* wasn't quite the right word. But his pupils were dilated, and he looked slightly unsettled, which was unusual for him.

And it had nothing to do with us. His expression didn't so much as flicker as he looked our way.

Someone had been here before us—someone who had startled the Devil himself.

Nah, I was being crazy.

The Devil's brows rose. "You brought an escort."

"Just a friend," Connor said.

I liked that his tone implied that I could take care of myself.

"Not just a friend." The Devil's gray eyes moved between us. "A mate."

Did I sense longing in his voice?

No—that was crazy.

He was so famous in Guild City that dozens of stories swirled around him. The one that had always stuck with me had come from a seer—that the Devil of Darkvale, the impossible ice man, would have his cold heart thawed by an outsider who would later betray him. It hadn't happened yet, and I didn't envy the person who was the other half of that prophecy.

Almost as if he'd read my thoughts, the Devil turned to ice. He'd already been a granite statue, so still and cold that he looked like rock. Now he could be mistaken for an impossibly perfect ice sculpture.

Yeah, I was being crazy. There was no one for the Devil.

"We brought the potion." I pulled it out of my pocket and approached.

Connor stuck by my side, not deviating an inch.

The Devil watched us keenly, a marble statue animated by intelligence and tightly leashed violence.

I set the potion on his desk, and he inspected it, picking it up to study it.

"It's perfect," Connor said.

"You made it?"

"Yes."

"Are you for hire?"

"If you vow to leave Sora alone and allow her to do whatever she wants in the city."

Warmth exploded within me. We'd known each other such a short time, but it felt like forever. It felt like there could *be* forever, if this was how he treated me.

"Agreed," the Devil said.

"And ensure that the Sorcerer's Guild doesn't seek retribution for what we took from them," Connor added. "I'm sure you have the power for that?"

The Devil merely inclined his head. "I do. And I will."

"Then feel free to call on me. Potions & Pastilles in Magic's Bend."

The Devil nodded once more, and it was clearly our cue.

We turned and left, but I couldn't help looking back at him. He seemed to have completely forgotten we were there and stared off into space. I shivered.

He was a cold bastard, and scary as hell. I reached for Connor's hand and gripped it tightly. Having him with me had proven one thing beyond a shadow of a doubt—he was the man for me. I could fight my own battles, but I could do so better with him.

The same hostess escorted us from the Devil's lair, and by the time we stepped out onto the street, I was grateful to be in the sunshine again. I pulled Connor down the road, away from the keen eyes of the bouncers. We slipped into an alley, and I turned to him, standing up on my tiptoes to press a kiss to his lips. "Thanks for having my back in there."

He pulled back and met my eyes. "I want to do more stuff like that for you. In the future, I mean."

"You want a future?"

"A future with a date in it, at least." Something flickered on his face, and though I couldn't identify it, I liked it. If it hadn't been so soon, I'd have almost said it looked something like love. "A lot of dates, I hope. All of them. Forever."

I grinned. "I could be cool with that, I think."

A cloud drifted over the sun, shrouding Guild City in darkness. "Will you come with me?"

"Anywhere."

I led him through the city to the street where my tiny flat was located. The road was narrow, and the two-story buildings were ancient, their second story protruding out over the road in the way that many medieval buildings did. I lived on the second floor, and I led him up to it, unlocking the door and stepping into the tiny one-room studio flat. The furniture was old and the smell a bit dusty.

I'd never loved it, but it had kept me dry. The best I could say was that I liked it pretty well, but that wasn't enough to make a life on.

"What are we doing here?" Connor asked.

"I just need to get something." There wasn't much in the flat that mattered to me, and maybe I would come back here one day. But I also liked the idea of leaving with Connor and having the option to keep on going. Not that I'd move in with him, or anything. But I wanted to see other things.

There was so much more to life than Guild City. It had

been my home, and an amazing one at that, but I hadn't had friends here. Or loved ones.

Being with Claire and Connor and Cass had made me see that. My uncontrollable magic had kept me apart from everyone here, and now that I had it back, maybe that could change.

But did I want it to?

Claire and Connor had liked me without it. I'd rather try my luck in Magic's Bend.

Quickly, I packed a bag with some books and clothes, making sure to gather up all the photos and mementos I could find. It didn't take me long, and soon I was ready.

"Let's go," I said.

Connor nodded and went to the door, leading the way down. We stepped out onto the street just as the three witches arrived.

Coraline, Mary, and Beth stared at us, their brows rising.

Beth smiled. "Perfect timing."

"We were coming to see you," Coraline said, her dark hair was streaked with blue today.

"We wanted to apologize," Beth said. "For trying to take your dagger. It was meant to be a prank, but it was uncool."

Mary shrugged one shoulder. "We're witches, but we didn't mean to be bitches."

"Wow. Um, thank you." It was nice of them, and it warmed me.

But still...

I looked at Connor. Once, I'd have killed for the

witches to be nice to me. But there was more out there. More than this, and I wanted to find it with him.

"I'll see you later," I said to the witches. Then I grabbed Connor's hand and pulled him down the street.

"What was all that about?" he asked.

"I'm not sure." I grinned and kissed him on the cheek. "Now, how about that date?"

~~

Want to know more about the Devil of Darkvale and the woman that Connor saw in Covent Garden? Hint—she's the reason the Devil was looking a bit shellshocked in the last scene. Their story, called *Once Bitten,* will be here at the end of April, so keep your eyes peeled.

THANK YOU FOR READING!

I hope you enjoyed reading this book as much as I enjoyed writing it. Reviews are *so* helpful to authors. I really appreciate all reviews, both positive and negative. If you want to leave one, you can do so at Amazon or GoodReads.

ACKNOWLEDGMENTS

Thank you, Ben, for everything. There would be no books without you.

Thank you to Jena O'Connor and Ash Fitzsimmons for your excellent editing. The book is immensely better because of you!

Thank you to Orina Kafe for the beautiful cover art.

AUTHOR'S NOTE

Hey there! I hope you enjoyed *Secrets and Alchemy*.

Most of the historical elements from this book were inspired by Dartmoor and a recent research trip to the UK with fellow author CN Crawford.

Dartmoor is full of amazing archaeological sites. One of the most remarkable are the Clapper Bridges, which can also be found on other upland areas of the UK. They are built of massive slabs of granite or schist laid over more stacked stones. Though they are generally thought to be prehistoric, many of them were built in the medieval period to facilitate crossing the rivers. The word 'clapper' comes from the Anglo-Saxon word *cleaca*, which means 'bridging the stepping stones'.

The small, gnarled trees that mark the entrance to the Court of Flames are based on Whistman's Wood, an ancient oak forest that is likely a holdover from before the deforestation of Dartmoor around 5000 BC. The ground there is so rocky that it was possibly never cleared, and many of the current stunted, twisted oaks are hundreds of years old.

Fletcher's Bar was inspired by the real life Gordon's Wine Bar, which is credited with being London's oldest wine bar (established 1890). While that is interesting, it is the building that I enjoyed the most. Check it out on Google to see photos of what I'm talking about—it's impossible to describe any better than I did in the text.

Thank you for coming along on Connor and Sora's adventure. Their book is finished for now, but there is always the possibility of another.

ABOUT LINSEY

Before becoming a writer, Linsey Hall was a nautical archaeologist who studied shipwrecks from Hawaii and the Yukon to the UK and the Mediterranean. She credits fantasy and historical romances with her love of history and her career as an archaeologist. After a decade of tromping around the globe in search of old bits of stuff that people left lying about, she settled down and started penning her own romance novels. Her Dragon's Gift series draws upon her love of history and the paranormal elements that she can't help but include.

COPYRIGHT

This is a work of fiction. All reference to events, persons, and locale are used fictitiously, except where documented in historical record. Names, characters, and places are products of the author's imagination, and any resemblance to actual events, locales, or persons, living or dead, is coincidental.
Copyright 2020 by Linsey Hall
Published by Bonnie Doon Press LLC
All rights reserved, including the right of reproduction in whole or in part in any form, except in instances of quotation used in critical articles or book review. Where such permission is sufficient, the author grants the right to strip any DRM which may be applied to this work.
Linsey@LinseyHall.com
www.LinseyHall.com
https://www.facebook.com/LinseyHallAuthor

Printed in Great Britain
by Amazon